Blackout!

Thunder boomed in the distance. A zigzag of lightning briefly lit up the dark lodge.

"We'd better get more light in here," Rene said. "Or people will get hurt. I just bumped into Jenny, and she said there were more candles in the basement."

"I'll go down to the basement," Stephanie said, "and you can pass out some of these flashlights." She handed half a dozen flashlights to Rene and grabbed a tall red candle for herself.

Stephanie took the steps down to the basement slowly. She could hear the thunder moving farther away as the storm's intensity decreased. *What was it that Mr. McCready said about a backup generator?* she wondered as her foot hit the back step. *If I could find it, maybe I could get the lights back on.*

Stephanie stood at the bottom of the steps and held the candle out in front of her so she could see where she needed to go. There was a door marked "Linens" and one had a sign that said "Janitorial Supplies." Which one would have candles?

Stephanie started down the hallway and saw there was a third room. She stepped forward.

A tall figure moved in the darkness, and Stephanie gasped in surprise. "Who—who is it?" she stammered.

"Who are you?" the figure replied.

FULL HOUSE™: Stephanie novels

Phone Call from a Flamingo
The Boy-Oh-Boy Next Door
Twin Troubles
Hip Hop Till You Drop
Here Comes the Brand-New Me
The Secret's Out
Daddy's Not-So-Little Girl
P.S. Friends Forever
Getting Even with the Flamingoes
The Dude of My Dreams
Back-to-School Cool
Picture Me Famous
Two-for-One Christmas Fun
The Big Fix-up Mix-up
Ten Ways to Wreck a Date
Wish Upon a VCR
Doubles or Nothing
Sugar and Spice Advice
Never Trust a Flamingo
The Truth About Boys
Crazy About the Future
My Secret Secret Admirer
Blue Ribbon Christmas
The Story on Older Boys
My Three Weeks as a Spy
No Business Like Show Business
Mail-Order Brother
To Cheat or Not to Cheat
Winning Is Everything
Hello Birthday, Good-bye Friend

The Art of Keeping Secrets
What Can You Grow on a Family
   Tree?
Girl Power

Club Stephanie:

#1 Fun, Sun, and Flamingoes
#2 Fireworks and Flamingoes
#3 Flamingo Revenge
#4 Too Many Flamingoes
#5 Friend or Flamingo?
#6 Flamingoes Overboard!
#7 Five Flamingo Summer
#8 Forget It, Flamingoes!
#9 Flamingoes Forever?
#10 Truth or Dare
#11 Summertime Secrets
#12 The Real Thing

Full House Sisters:

Two on the Town
One Boss Too Many
And the Winner Is . . .
Problems in Paradise
How to Hide a Horse
Will You Be My Valentine?
Let's Put on a Show

Available from MINSTREL Books

FULL HOUSE™ CLUB
Stephanie

The Real Thing
Based on the hit Warner Bros. TV series

Kathy Clark

A Parachute Press Book

A MINSTREL® BOOK

Published by POCKET BOOKS
New York London Toronto Sydney Singapore

A MINSTREL PAPERBACK *Original*

A Minstrel Book published by
POCKET BOOKS, a division of Simon & Schuster Inc.
1230 Avenue of the Americas, New York, NY 10020

A PARACHUTE PRESS BOOK

Copyright © and ™ 2000 by Warner Bros.

ISBN: 0-671-04193-2

First Minstrel Books printing August 2000

10 9 8 7 6 5 4 3 2 1

CHAPTER
1

◆ ◀ ◖ ◆

Stephanie Tanner raced across the beach to the edge of Camp Sail-Away's lake and stopped short. Out on the lake, two Windsurfers were wobbling toward each other. The girls on them were not paying attention.

"Tammy! Marguerite! Look up! You're about to crash!" Stephanie called to the girls on the Windsurfers.

Good thing I came down here dressed to swim, Stephanie thought. She tossed her T-shirt and towel on the sand, jumped in the lake, and started swimming. Just as she approached the girls, Marguerite veered abruptly away from Tammy.

1

But the near-crash was enough to make both girls lose their balance and fall into the water.

"Look out for the Windsurfers!" Stephanie shouted to the two ten-year-old girls. She grabbed one of the Windsurfers to keep it from hitting the girls.

"Whoa! Sorry, Stephanie," Marguerite Hansen said. The straps of her black and silver swimsuit sparkled in the midday sun. Small and pretty, she pushed her short blond hair off her face.

"Thanks for catching my board!" Tammy Walters called as she stood up and waded through the water on her long brown legs. She was tall and athletic, with an open, friendly smile. Both Tammy and Marguerite lived in Loon Cabin, where Stephanie was a counselor-in-training or CIT. *Or used to be,* she thought in frustration. *Until yesterday.*

"You guys need more help?" Stephanie said as she moved toward Tammy and Marguerite.

"Please," Tammy said.

"Well, all I can offer is to tell you to get back up there," Stephanie said with a laugh. She squeezed water out of her long, blond ponytail. She put a hand above her blue eyes to shield them from the sun and gazed out at the lake.

"Do you see Luke out there in his motorboat?" Marguerite asked as she pulled the second Windsurfer toward Stephanie. Tammy had managed to get back on and was sailing away from them.

Stephanie shook her head. But Marguerite had read her mind. Stephanie was keeping an eye out for him. Luke Hayes had been her boyfriend—until he was kicked out of Camp Clearwater, Camp Sail-Away's brother camp.

"Too bad," Marguerite said. "I'd really like to talk to him, you know? I don't think I thanked him enough yesterday."

Stephanie thought back to the camp's Silly Sailboat Race the day before. What a disaster! Marguerite had been racing when she capsized and almost drowned. Stephanie tried to rescue her, but Marguerite's heavy costume nearly dragged them to the bottom of the lake. Luckily, Luke showed up in his motorboat and saved them both.

But Stephanie wasn't allowed to talk to Luke since he'd been expelled from camp. She lost her CIT position for breaking that rule—even though he'd rescued her and Marguerite. It was so unfair!

Stephanie felt sad thinking of her adorable,

blond, blue-eyed Luke. Something about him was so . . . right for her. They'd only been dating a week or so when someone vandalized the boys' camp lodge, and all the signs pointed to its being Luke. He'd been accused of cutting loose all of Camp Clearwater's boats one night the summer before. He lost his CIT privileges for that. This year he was kicked out of camp even though he said he didn't vandalize the lodge. *And I believe him,* Stephanie thought.

"I don't think I thanked him enough, either," Stephanie told Marguerite. *I hugged him, and I told him I'd clear his name and get him readmitted to camp. But is that enough? Not until I actually do all the things I promised.*

"Maybe we could get a boat and go find Luke together," Marguerite suggested. "He lives around here, right? You said his family has a cabin on the lake, so all we have to do is—"

Stephanie smiled at Marguerite and patted the Windsurfer. "Are you going to sail this thing today or what?"

"Okay, okay—I'm going!" Marguerite laughed and carefully climbed back on her board. She slowly got to her feet and grabbed the sail bar.

Stephanie smiled to herself, glad that she and

Marguerite were finally getting along. Marguerite's older sister Cynthia was a member of a club called the Flamingoes—the same club Stephanie had refused to join back in the sixth grade. Ever since then, the Flamingoes had made it their business to be mean to Stephanie and her friends. Cynthia had told Marguerite she hated Stephanie—so Marguerite copied her big sister and hated Stephanie, too.

But that changed after Stephanie had tried to rescue Marguerite the day before. Suddenly Marguerite seemed to think that everything Stephanie did was perfect.

Stephanie held the Windsurfer steady for Marguerite. "Okay, set your feet apart. Now, what you want to do is—"

"No, no, no!"

Stephanie turned around to see Heather O'Donnell standing above them on the dock. Heather was the assistant camp director. She wore crease-less khaki shorts and a green Camp Sail-Away staff polo shirt that looked as if it had been ironed. Her short brown hair curled perfectly around the shirt collar.

"Am I doing something wrong?" Stephanie asked, surprised. She'd taught a lot of kids to windsurf, and no one ever challenged her about it before. "She has to grab the sail," Stephanie argued.

"Well, yes, of course," Heather admitted. "You know exactly what you're doing. The problem is, this is against camp regulations. You're not a CIT anymore, Stephanie," she said firmly. "You no longer teach water sports!"

"I wasn't teaching a class," Stephanie said, stung by Heather's words. "I was just helping Tammy and Marguerite—"

"I'm sorry, Stephanie. But you'll have to leave the teaching to the counselors from now on," Heather said.

Stephanie couldn't help noticing that Heather didn't sound very sorry about it at all.

"But we like it when Stephanie helps us," Marguerite piped up. "Before Stephanie came over to help us, Tammy and I almost crashed into each other." She slipped off the Windsurfer into the lake. "Please don't fire her," Marguerite pleaded. "It's a really dumb idea."

Heather's eyes widened. "Oh, is that so?" She sounded surprised.

"Marguerite!" Stephanie whispered. "Shh!"

Marguerite ignored Stephanie's warning. She

arched one eyebrow and gave Heather a very snobby look. "Stephanie saved my life. She's the best CIT at camp. When I tell my daddy that you fired her, he'll . . . he'll . . . he'll ask for his money back!"

"Sorry, Heather," Stephanie interrupted. She gently tried to push Marguerite aside. "Marguerite's just upset." She didn't want Marguerite to get into trouble, too.

Heather frowned. "No one's getting their money back. Now, Stephanie. As you may have guessed, you'll be moving out of Loon Cabin," she said briskly. "I see you've signed up for all three two-week sessions. Since camp is full right now, you can stay in Loon Cabin until this session ends next Sunday—one week from today. But you'll be spending the last session in Brown Bear Cabin." Heather turned and marched across the sand to talk to a counselor teaching swimming.

Stephanie's heart sank as she watched Heather go. She didn't want to move out of Loon Cabin. She had been hoping she could stay in the same cabin, even if she wasn't the CIT there. She walked out of the water and picked up her T-shirt and towel from the beach.

"Stephanie, I don't want you to move out!"

Marguerite cried as she dragged the Windsurfer out of the water.

Tammy zipped toward the shore and jumped off her Windsurfer. "You're moving out?" she asked.

"I lost my CIT job," Stephanie said.

"Heather's making her move," Marguerite explained.

"Who's going to tell us ghost stories that make our skin crawl?" Tammy asked. "Who's going to clean up after we clean up—so we don't get in trouble?"

"I never did that," Stephanie said with a laugh.

"Oh. Well, maybe that was just wishful thinking," Tammy admitted. "But you were a really good CIT. You almost had us winning the Silly Sailboat Race."

"Come on, Stephanie—please don't move," Marguerite begged. "I know, we'll start a petition. Everyone in the cabin can sign it."

"Thanks, but I don't think that'll work. Believe me, I don't want to move, but . . ." Stephanie shrugged. "I guess I'll have to. I'm not a CIT anymore."

"We've got to do something. I don't know what, but . . . we'll find a way," Marguerite promised.

Stephanie grinned at her. "Why do I get the feeling you will?"

But no matter how much her campers believed in her, Stephanie didn't think she would ever be a CIT again. Heather didn't trust her.

Stephanie knew there was only one solution to the mess she was in. She had to clear Luke's name—and her own! *If Luke is innocent, then talking to him wouldn't be wrong,* she thought. *I'll track down the person who really trashed the boys' lodge.*

But how?

CHAPTER
2

◆ ◂ ▸ ◆

"Greetings, Camp Sail-Away girls! I have an announcement to make." Mr. McCready's voice boomed over the clang and clatter of dishes being cleared. The camp director was standing on the small stage in the lodge Sunday night. The lodge was the large wooden log building where campers ate all their meals and had social events.

Stephanie had just finished eating dinner with the campers in Loon Cabin. Now she was sitting with all her CIT friends for dessert.

Darcy Powell darted over to Stephanie's chair and crouched beside her. "I wonder what the big announcement is!" Darcy wore a white sleeveless shirt and faded blue jean shorts. Her dark brown hair was pulled back under a headband.

"Maybe Mr. McCready's going to say that he changed his mind about Stephanie. Maybe he's going to let Stephanie be a CIT again," Allie Taylor suggested as she pushed up the sleeves of her sweatshirt. Allie and Stephanie had been best friends for years.

Stephanie rolled her eyes. "Yeah, right. I don't think he'd make an announcement like that in front of the whole camp. Besides, it's not going to happen."

"Hey, it could happen," Anna Rice said as she ate the last bite of her brownie sundae. Anna's silver bracelets jangled on her freckled arm as she lifted the spoon to her mouth.

"And it will," Kayla Norris predicted. She flipped her long blond hair over her shoulder. "I know you, Stephanie. You're not going to give up!"

Stephanie smiled. "No, probably not. You know what? My campers told Heather that she made a mistake."

"Heather? Make a mistake?" Allie gasped. "Never!"

"Well, it's not like she'd ever admit it, anyway," Darcy said.

"Attention, attention!" Heather clanged a large metal spoon against the table. "Could we please have it quiet?"

Stephanie looked up at Heather and Mr. McCready.

"Returning campers probably know what this is all about," Mr. McCready began. "We're reaching the end of this session, which means it's time for a very special event. This is usually the highlight of every summer. Yes, I'm talking about our Camp Sail-Away Talent Show!"

Everyone in the lodge whooped and hollered.

"Each cabin will perform an act of their own choosing," Mr. McCready explained. "Naturally, our friends over at Camp Clearwater will be here to watch the show."

Stephanie looked at Allie. "That means Sam will be watching you!" she whispered with a broad grin. Allie had started dating Sam about a week ago. Stephanie thought they made a really cute couple.

Allie wiggled her eyebrows. "I hope so. Unless I totally embarrass myself."

"You won't," Kayla assured her.

Mr. McCready continued. "Heather and I will be judges, along with a few counselors from the boys' camp, just to keep things impartial. We'll award prizes to the best acts."

"This sounds like so much fun," Anna said.

Stephanie nodded in agreement. She loved talent shows.

"So, now all we need is a show and stage manager." Mr. McCready gazed out at the crowd. "Every year we select a senior camper to do the job."

There were murmurs all around the dining room as everyone reacted to the news.

"I know our counselors and CITs could do it," Mr. McCready said. "But we like to give someone else at camp a special chance to get involved. This is an all-camper production, run by and starring you guys. The way we do this is to ask you all to nominate someone—and then we vote." Mr. McCready smiled as he rubbed his hands together. "Don't be shy. Speak right up. Would anyone like to make a nomination?"

Across the dining room Stephanie saw Marguerite spring to her feet. She nearly knocked over her chair. "I nominate Stephanie Tanner," she declared.

Stephanie didn't know what to say. Everyone in the dining room was looking at her now. She smiled at Marguerite. "Thanks," she mouthed.

urse you should have that job!" Anna
edly. "It makes perfect sense."

r of Stephanie's former campers got to
her feet. "I totally agree with Marguerite," Vanessa
said. "Stephanie would put on a great show."

Heather peered down at her from the stage and
frowned. "In other words, you second the nomination? Is that what you're trying to say?"

Everyone in Loon Cabin stood up. "We all second the nomination," Tammy announced in a
firm voice.

Darcy leaned over to whisper in Stephanie's
ear. "Heather looks like she just bit into a lemon!"

Stephanie covered her mouth to keep from
laughing out loud. Heather did look miserable.
Stephanie knew it was only a matter of time
before she told everyone that Stephanie couldn't
take the job. She wasn't in good standing with
Heather or Mr. McCready. They'd never let her
have that much responsibility.

"Well, er . . . how about some other names?"
Mr. McCready looked around the dining room.

Nobody said anything for a minute. Stephanie
watched as campers at a table next to her con-
ferred. *I wonder who else is going to want the job*, she
thought. *I know someone will.*

Behind her she heard a chair being pushed back. She turned and saw Jasmine James, a girl from Brown Bear Cabin where Stephanie used to live. She'd be moving back in there in a week, according to Heather.

"Excuse me, Mr. McCready? Heather?" Jasmine asked politely.

"Yes, Jasmine!" Heather nearly shouted. "Do you have another name to submit to us? Would you like to nominate yourself?"

"No, not me. I just want to say that I think Stephanie would do a great job," Jasmine said. "And everyone at this table agrees with me. So we third that nomination." Jasmine looked at Stephanie and smiled.

Stephanie felt her face turn red. Jasmine was so nice! Stephanie couldn't believe how wonderful it was to have everyone's support. Just when she was feeling really awful about losing her CIT job, here were her friends sticking up for her—again.

"Let's go ahead and vote!" Tammy called out.

"Now, wait a minute. Are there any more nominations? Isn't there anyone else who wants to be the talent show manager?" Heather asked.

"We're holding the vote tonight, so if anyone is interested, please let us know—now," Mr.

McCready added. He surveyed the room one more time. "As I said, there's no need to be shy." He let out a nervous laugh.

He turned to the table where the Flamingoes were sitting. Rene Salter, the leader of the group, suddenly jumped to her feet. "I nominate Tiffany Schroeder!" she cried. Tiffany was the only Flamingo who wasn't a CIT.

"What?" Tiffany scoffed. "No way!"

"But Tiffany, you've got to do it," Rene told her. "Think of how much fun we'll have."

Tiffany shook her head. "Mr. McCready, I'm sorry, but please withdraw my name. It sounds like way too much work." She fluffed her blond hair.

Allie and Kayla snickered. "Tiffany hates work," Anna added with a grin. "Forget about any competition from her."

"All right, Tiffany's not on the list," Mr. McCready agreed. "The person who takes on this job needs to be ready to work hard. And that person would be . . ." He waited for any other nominations. He turned to Heather, and she shrugged.

"I guess that's the end of the nomination period, Mr. M," she said.

"Stephanie! You're the only one running." Darcy squeezed her arm. "It's in the bag."

"All right, then. May I see a show of hands for Stephanie Tanner?" Mr. McCready finally asked.

Stephanie gasped as almost everyone in the dining room raised her hand. Stephanie didn't think she should vote for herself, so she didn't put her hand in the air.

"Against?" he asked.

Rene, Tiffany, Darah Judson, and Jenny Lyons— all Flamingoes—raised their hands.

But Cynthia Hansen, Marguerite's sister, didn't. Stephanie couldn't believe that Cynthia wasn't voting with the rest of the Flamingoes.

Rene nudged Cynthia's arm and tried to get her to vote with them, but she wouldn't. Both Rene and Darah glared at her.

Is Cynthia not voting against me? Stephanie wondered. *Just because of what I did to save Marguerite?*

"Let's see." Mr. McCready scratched his head. "That would be . . ."

"I think I have the accurate count. One hundred twelve for Stephanie and four against," Heather said.

"You got it, Steph!" Darcy cried as she gave Stephanie a high five. "The job's yours!"

Stephanie glowed with excitement. *I can't*

believe it, she thought. *I'm going to manage the talent show! That's almost as good as being a CIT.*

"We'd like to welcome Stephanie as our new show manager." Heather looked as if she were trying to smile, but her mouth hardly moved. "I'll meet with you in a few minutes, Stephanie. Please wait for me. I also need to speak with all of the CITs, so don't run off."

"Sure thing! Thanks, Heather." Stephanie stood up and waved at her and then at all of the tables. "Thanks, everyone!"

Seconds later a crowd of girls surrounded Stephanie and bombarded her with questions.

"Can I do a solo act?"

"Are we going to have live music?"

"Can we do anything we want?"

Stephanie held up her hands in protest. "I don't know all the details yet, guys! Let me go talk to Heather and I'll fill you in tomorrow, okay?" She managed to work her way out of the crowd toward Heather. Her friends followed closely behind her.

"Thanks for letting me do this, Heather," Stephanie said. "I promise I'll do a really good job. I won't let you down."

"No, you won't," Heather said. "Because I won't allow that to happen. And if all those

18

campers believe in you . . . well then, maybe I can, too. Eventually."

That wasn't much of a compliment, but coming from Heather, it was something. "So how does this work?" Stephanie asked. "Am I allowed to ask anyone to help me, or—"

"Of course. Don't be ridiculous. Nobody could do that job all on her own." Heather brushed at an imaginary crumb on her shorts. "Of course, I did, back when they let counselors be in charge."

Anna poked Stephanie in the ribs. "I'm sure she did," she whispered.

"She's probably the reason counselors aren't allowed to run it anymore," Kayla added with a giggle.

Heather cleared her throat and stared at her. "What was that, girls?"

"Oh, nothing," Kayla said. "We were just hoping we could help Stephanie."

Heather nodded. "Very good guess. Actually, part of Stephanie's job is organizing all the counselors-in-training. You're the ones who will help her run a fantastic, error-free show."

"That sounds great," Anna said.

"Awesome," Kayla agreed with a nod. "I can't wait."

"What were you saying, Heather? We didn't hear you exactly," Rene said as she walked up, followed by the rest of the Flamingoes. Rene pushed up the sleeves of her heavy pink sweatshirt.

"I was telling Stephanie that all the CITs will work with her on the talent show. She has to organize it and be the stage manager," Heather told the Flamingoes. "But you guys will help her put on a fabulous show."

"What? We will?" Darah put her hand over her heart.

"How incredibly lucky for us." Rene shot Stephanie a wicked smile.

"Meet me in my office tomorrow morning at nine sharp," Heather continued. "We'll map out a plan of who does what."

"Gee, I can't wait," Jenny said with a pointed look at Stephanie.

"We sure would love to do whatever we can," Rene said. "Anything to help Stephanie."

"Right . . ." Heather seemed confused by the Flamingoes' sudden change in attitude. "Didn't you just cast the only votes against Stephanie?"

"I didn't," Cynthia said.

Rene frowned at her. "Yeah, I remember."

"Well, anyway," Cynthia said, "we can all come

together for the good of the talent show. Right, guys?"

"Definitely," Rene assured Heather with a phony nod.

"Then it's one for all, all for one," Heather declared. "However, if anything goes wrong, Stephanie, I'll hold you personally responsible. See you girls tomorrow at nine—I need to go organize the kitchen storage shelves. Rene and Tiffany, I'll see you at the dishwashing machine in five minutes!"

Rene and Tiffany were on probation, and dishwashing was part of their punishment. They had been caught sneaking out at night to go canoeing with Keith and Tyler, two boys from Camp Clearwater.

After Heather walked off, Rene turned to Jenny. "I can't believe you couldn't pull some strings and get me out of this," she said. "Being on probation is the pits!" She ran a hand through her short brown hair.

"I'm sorry," Jenny said. "I asked my dad to change his mind, but he wouldn't." Jenny's stepfather was Mr. McCready. She was covered in Camp Sail-Away gear, from the baseball cap over her wavy brown hair to her socks. "Anyway, it's only for a week, right?"

"That's long enough." Rene shook her head and looked at Stephanie. "And I can't believe you told Mr. McCready on us."

"You were accusing me of sneaking out to see Luke!" Stephanie cried. "Which I wasn't."

"Whatever," Rene said. "Do you realize how many extra chores I have to do now?"

"Hey, at least you're still a CIT!" Stephanie said.

"As if I have time to be," Rene shot back. "I'm too busy doing all the chores they've saved up for the last twenty years. All because of you!"

Stephanie shrugged. "I never told you to sneak out in the canoe with Keith and Tyler. That was your idea."

"That reminds me. Keith hates me now. So thanks for that, too." Rene glowered at Stephanie. "I'll never forget this, Stephanie. And I don't know how I'll pay you back, but I will, before the summer's over—you can count on that!"

I won't listen to her, Stephanie thought. *I'm going to direct the talent show, and nothing Rene can do will ruin that.*

I hope!

CHAPTER
3

◆ ◀ ◗ ◆

Heather glanced at the clock above her desk. It was Monday morning at nine. "Rene had better hurry," Heather grumbled. "We need to start planning this talent show. You can never do too much planning. That's what I always say."

Stephanie looked around the room at her friends and tried not to smile. For once she agreed with Heather. She couldn't wait to start planning the show.

Cynthia shrugged. "We could always start without her," she suggested.

"No way," Darah replied. "Rene has to be here. Are you crazy?"

"Well, all I can say is that she needs to learn how

to get places on time," Heather said. "Because promptness is—"

Just then Stephanie heard loud footsteps on the stairs. "It's about time," Heather commented as she tapped her fingers against the desk.

Rene pushed open the door and walked into the office. There were pieces of hay sticking out of her hair, and she had mud all over her hiking boots.

Tiffany came in right behind her. Dirt covered her face, and one of her T-shirt sleeves was torn.

"Sorry we're late," Rene mumbled as she slid into a chair.

"What happened to you two?" Heather asked. Everyone else was just staring at Rene and Tiffany, completely dumbfounded.

"We had to clean out the horse stables. Remember?" Rene asked with a pointed look at Heather. "From seven until nine."

"Oh, that's where you were." Darah shook her head. "I couldn't figure out why you didn't show for breakfast."

"You guys didn't get breakfast?" Jenny asked, concerned.

"Of course they ate breakfast. I left some muffins and fresh fruit down at the stables for them," Heather said.

Rene glared at her. "The horses ate them."

"Oh. Well, I'll get you something from the kitchen," Heather said. "I didn't mean for you to go hungry. Was it a lot of work?"

"You could say that." Tiffany rubbed her arm. "I'm sore!"

"It was going fine until one of the horses escaped," Rene explained. "Don't worry, we got her back. But we were running after her, and we fell, and—"

"Oh, so that explains the smell." Darah put her hand over her nose and started to giggle.

Rene frowned at her. "Ha ha, very funny."

"You *are* sort of stinking up my office," Heather said. She got up and opened both of the windows. "Well then, to save our noses, let's make this meeting short. Tiffany, if you want to head downstairs, I'm sure there are some leftover muffins in the kitchen—"

"I don't want to leave," Tiffany said. "I mean, I came along with Rene because I need to ask you a big favor."

"Yes?" Heather waited patiently as Tiffany pulled a long piece of straw out of her hair.

"Would you please let me help with the talent show?" Tiffany asked. "I know I'm not a CIT, and

I'm not supposed to, but all my friends are CITs and I feel left out." She sniffled. "I couldn't even sleep last night, I was so miserable."

Darcy looked over at Stephanie and rolled her eyes.

Stephanie smiled. Tiffany was known for being a little on the dramatic side.

"I'll consider it," Heather said. "What special skills could you offer?"

"Well, I've been in three talent shows and two beauty pageants," Tiffany bragged. "I even won once. And I know a ton about all the backstage stuff."

"Hmm. Very impressive. All right, you can participate," Heather told her. "The more the merrier, right, Stephanie? You need all the help you can get."

Stephanie smiled unevenly. Tiffany wasn't exactly known for her helpfulness. *Still,* Stephanie thought, *maybe this time she'll have a few ideas.*

Heather tapped a stack of colored index cards against her desk. "We have lots to accomplish this morning. Stephanie, let's get started. I can give you some helpful tips from the year I organized the talent show."

Stephanie sighed as she stared at the index

cards. Heather had a way of taking the fun out of everything.

"So, do you think you can take it from here?" Heather asked about fifteen minutes later.

Stephanie glanced at her hastily scribbled list and nodded. "I think I'm all set. Thanks a lot!"

"You're welcome," Heather said. "I have to run—I need to supervise a hike. You girls can see yourselves out, can't you? Oh, before I go—Mr. M and I decided to make this year's talent show a fundraiser, for the local kids."

"What a great idea!" Stephanie said enthusiastically.

"We thought so," Heather said. "So the first thing you'll need to do is sell tickets to all the boys from Camp Clearwater. I suggest you do it at lunch tomorrow—choose two shifts."

"We'll take the first shift," Rene volunteered.

"Okay, great. We'll take the second," Stephanie said.

"I'll give Stephanie the tickets and the cash box tomorrow," Heather said. "And explain all the details. Some of the boys might resist buying the tickets, since we've never charged before. But I'm sure they'll come around."

"Sounds great," Stephanie said.

"Oh, no, now I'm going to be late." Heather grabbed her green fleece jacket from a coat hook. "Stephanie, get everyone to sign up for something—pronto!" She rushed out the door.

Stephanie looked around at everyone. "So, I have a list of assignments here. How about if I read them off, and you guys volunteer?"

"What if more than one person wants the job? Are you automatically going to give it to your friends, over us?" Darah asked in a snobby tone.

"No, of course not," Stephanie said. *That might be the way the Flamingoes work—but I'll be fair.* "We can use two people on any one of these jobs, anyway. Okay, first off—music. Who wants to be in charge of setting up music, playing CDs, and stuff like that?"

Darcy raised a hand. "I do."

Cynthia put her hand in the air, too. "So do I."

"Okay, Darcy and Cynthia will be our DJs." Stephanie jotted that down on her list. "Now, sets and design."

"I'd like to do that," Jenny offered.

"So would I," Anna said.

"Great! Next we have makeup," Stephanie said. "Anyone?"

"Me me me!" Tiffany cried.

"I'll help," Allie said.

"Costumes, clothes, whatever people end up wearing?" Stephanie asked.

Both Darah and Kayla signed up for that job.

"The only thing left is lighting," Stephanie said. "Rene? Would you be willing to help me with that? It sort of goes along with stage direction, but—"

"Oh, no problem," Rene said. "Lighting is incredibly important. It can make or break an act. Right?"

"Definitely," Stephanie agreed. She couldn't believe how much the Flamingoes were pitching in. Apparently they wanted to do a good job and impress Heather as much as she did. *That's going to make this so much easier!* she thought. "Okay then. Meeting adjourned. We'll start painting a set this afternoon, and tomorrow we'll ask cabins to sign up and let us know what kind of acts they're planning. Okay?"

"Sure," Rene said as all of her friends rose from their chairs. "But there's just one slight problem." She paused in the doorway.

"Oh? What's that?" Stephanie asked casually.

"The fact that we're not going to help you with anything!" Rene said.

She, Jenny, Darah, and Tiffany all started laughing. Then they filed out the door and down the hall. Stephanie could hear them laugh all the way out of the lodge.

Cynthia stayed behind for a second. "Sorry." She looked at Stephanie and shrugged. "I'm sure Rene didn't really mean that. We're going to help—or at least I am."

"Thanks," Stephanie told her.

Then Cynthia took off after her friends.

"Do you think Cynthia's right?" Stephanie wondered out loud. "Are they going to help? You heard what Rene said last night about paying me back for getting her on probation."

"Don't worry, Steph. We'll make this work—with their help or without it," Allie declared.

"Anyway, you have all the campers behind you. They'll make sure you put on a good show," Darcy said.

"You're right," Stephanie agreed as she got more excited about the show. "Forget about Rene and her dumb threat. We'll put on a great show—without her."

"Exactly," Anna agreed.

"So what did you want to pick up today?" Allie asked. She and Stephanie were walking down the main street in town that Monday afternoon. With them was Marguerite, who had begged to come along.

"We need some makeup, and some paint for the sets, and anything else you can think of. Heather gave me a budget," Stephanie explained. "It's not much of one, but it'll help."

"I'm going to buy some new barrettes at the drugstore," Marguerite said. "I think I've lost half of mine in the lake. I keep forgetting to take them out before I dive in."

"I hate when that happens," Allie told her. She reached up to fasten a silver butterfly barrette in her hair. "Is it still in there? Oh, good."

"If anyone ever drains the lake, they'll probably find a few thousand barrettes at the bottom," Stephanie said.

"So, Stephanie," Marguerite said with a sly smile. "How do you like my plan? Think it will work?"

Stephanie stared at her, confused. "What plan?"

"To make you a CIT again," Marguerite explained. "That's why I nominated you to be the head of the talent show. When Mr. McCready sees what a cool show you're going to do, he'll *beg* you to be a CIT again. On his knees!"

Allie and Stephanie laughed. "Thanks, Marguerite," Stephanie said. "I hope your plan works. But even if it doesn't, I can't wait to work on the show. So I can't lose!"

She pushed open the door to a small drugstore. A bell jingled as they entered.

"Come on—the makeup's back there." Marguerite tugged on Stephanie's sleeve.

Allie and Stephanie compared eye crayons and face powder for a few minutes. Allie couldn't decide what they needed more—she'd never done stage makeup before.

"If only Tiffany the pageant expert were here, she could tell us what to get," Allie said.

"Let's get some lipstick. We definitely need that," Stephanie said. "But which colors?"

Marguerite let out a bored sigh. "I'm going to check out the hair stuff," she announced. She started to walk away, and Stephanie heard the bell over the drugstore door jingle again as the door opened.

Marguerite came running back toward Stephanie. "Look! Look who just came in!" She pointed to the front of the store, near the cash register.

Stephanie stepped to the side so she could see past Marguerite. *Is that who I think it is?*

"Uh-oh," Allie said as she came up behind Stephanie. "It's Luke!"

CHAPTER
4

◆ ◀ ◆ ◆

Stephanie's heart beat fiercely at the sight of Luke. His sun-streaked blond hair fell almost into his eyes. He wore long tan cargo shorts, a blue T-shirt, and sandals. He was tall and his long legs were tanned from his being outdoors and on the lake all summer long.

Luke turned and his eyes met Stephanie's. She felt her cheeks redden. *He just caught me staring at him.* She waved awkwardly, then hurried up to the front of the store. Her friends followed.

Luke grinned as she got closer. He looked as happy to see her as she was to see him. "Hi, Stephanie," he said warmly. "Hi, Marguerite and Allie."

"How are you?" Marguerite asked. "It is so cool that you're here. Stephanie and I were talking about you yesterday."

Marguerite, shut up, Stephanie thought in embarrassment.

Luke raised his eyebrows. "Oh, really?"

"Yeah," Marguerite said.

"And what were you saying?" Luke turned to Stephanie again with a mischievous smile.

"We were talking about how you saved me," Marguerite said. "And how we wished we could see you again so we could thank you."

Luke tapped his fingers against a map display. "What a coincidence. I was hoping I'd see you guys again, too."

Allie shrugged. "Then this must be one of those psychic coincidences you hear about. Right, Steph?"

"I don't know about that," Stephanie said. "I mean, this is a pretty small town. We're bound to run into each other. Right?"

"Let's see . . . considering you guys come into town about once a week? I'd say meeting you here is kind of lucky!" Luke laughed. "At least for me. So what are you doing here? Stocking up?" He pointed to the dozen or so lipsticks in

Stephanie's hands and grinned. "I didn't know you wore that much."

Stephanie laughed. "They're not for me," she told him.

"We're buying makeup for the camp talent show," Allie said. "Stephanie was appointed stage manager yesterday."

"Isn't that cool?" Marguerite asked. "You have to come see the show."

"Wait a second," Luke said. "Don't they give that job to a camper who's not a CIT?" His forehead creased with concern as he gazed into Stephanie's eyes.

"Guess who lost her CIT job," Allie said as she gave Luke a disapproving look.

"It's all Heather's fault," Marguerite added.

"What?" Luke asked. "Wait—it's not Heather, is it? It's all because of me."

"You could say that," Allie said.

"Allie!" Stephanie cried. "It's not Luke's fault."

Allie didn't stop, though. "Heather warned Stephanie she couldn't see you again. And when she saw you on the lake during the sailboat race, she figured you guys planned to meet out there."

"What?" Luke cried. "That's ridiculous. We

never planned anything. Stephanie, let me talk to her—"

"It won't work." Stephanie shook her head. "Her mind is made up." *And what's more, she won't believe a word you say*, she thought to herself.

"Do you guys mind if we talk in private for a second?" Luke asked Marguerite and Allie.

"I don't mind," Marguerite said.

"But make it short," Allie warned. "If anyone sees you guys together, Stephanie could lose her stage manager job."

"Don't worry," Luke said in an irritated voice. "I won't ruin anything else for Stephanie this summer." He took Stephanie's arm and guided her into an aisle where books and magazines were displayed. "I feel so lousy about what's happened," he said. "You must hate me."

Stephanie shook her head and looked up into Luke's eyes. "I don't hate you." *Allie might*, she thought. *But I definitely don't.*

"You don't?" Luke met her gaze, and Stephanie felt a shiver go through her. The connection between them was so intense.

"No. I could never hate you," she told Luke, her voice barely a whisper.

Luke traced her cheek with his hand. "Not after

everything that's happened? First I get booted from camp, then I make you lose your CIT position—"

"That wasn't your fault," Stephanie said. "Anyway, if I can, I'm going to prove you never did anything wrong, and you shouldn't have been asked to leave camp in the first place. And if I can prove that, you can come back, and I'll be a CIT again."

"Wow." Luke took a step back. "You sound really determined."

"I am," Stephanie said. "Don't ask me how I'll do it, though." She wrinkled her nose. "I haven't exactly figured that out."

"But you will." Luke grinned. "Somehow I know that. Hey, so when's the talent show? How did you swing that job?"

"It's this Saturday. Marguerite nominated me," Stephanie said. "And then—"

"Steph! Luke!" Allie cried. "Someone's coming."

The doorbell jingled, and Stephanie started to walk away from Luke. She wasn't afraid of seeing anyone except Heather or Mr. McCready. But with her luck lately, the person entering the store could easily be one of the two!

"Oh, it's only you," she heard Allie say.

"Great to see you, too," a male voice answered.

Stephanie stepped out of the magazine aisle. Luke was right behind her.

"It's cool, Stephanie—it's just Keith," Luke said in a soft voice.

Just Keith? Stephanie looked at Allie and raised an eyebrow. Luke had no idea what had gone on with Keith lately. He didn't know how angry Keith was with Stephanie. She'd turned him in for sneaking out at night in a canoe with Rene—and he ended up on probation. He hadn't spoken to her since.

"Hey, Keith—how's it going?" Luke greeted him in a friendly tone. Luke and Keith were both fifteen, and had both been going to Camp Clearwater for the past few years.

"I'm on probation, man—how do you think it's going?" Keith cracked a bitter smile at Stephanie, then shifted some shopping bags in his arms. "I'm running errands for Mr. Davis."

Stephanie stared uncomfortably at the tips of her sneakers.

"On probation?" Luke asked. "Why?"

Keith shook his head. "All I can say is, stay away from those Sail-Away girls. They'll get you into trouble every time."

Stephanie tried to laugh at Keith's sort-of joke, but it came out more like a cough.

"Hey—it's not our fault you broke the rules," Marguerite cut in.

"Maybe not," Keith admitted, grinning tensely at Stephanie. "But it *is* your fault I got caught!"

Luke glanced at Stephanie. "Is everything cool between you guys?"

"Sure," Stephanie muttered. "About as cool as an iceberg."

Keith moved the shopping bags over to his hip. "This stuff is getting heavy. Errand boy has got to go—"

"Hey, I like your shirt," Marguerite commented with a nod.

Stephanie looked at Keith's T-shirt. It was navy blue with a white moon on the front and back. It said "Clearwater Midnight Moonlight Sail" in big letters under the moon's image.

"A bunch of guys have them." Keith tugged on the hem of the T-shirt. "Me, Luke, Max—"

"We did this midnight race a few years back," Luke explained. "Only a few of us, the best sailors at camp. It was so cool. Except the wind died right at midnight, and we were all stuck on the lake for hours."

Marguerite giggled. "Why don't they do that every year?"

Keith shook his head. "They canceled it. They love to cancel the fun stuff," he said with a bite in his voice. "Hey, no one goes to camp for *fun*, right?"

Marguerite laughed. Stephanie made that little coughing noise again.

Stephanie wondered if he was just mad about being on probation, or if something else was bothering him.

"So what kind of errands are you running, Keith? Buying souvenirs?" Luke joked as he pointed at the shopping bags. "Man, what did you do, buy out the town?" He reached for one of the bags.

Keith jerked away from him. "Hands off!"

"What's the big deal?" Luke asked. "Is it a secret?"

"For now? Yeah. This stuff is for my act in the talent show," Keith said.

"You guys have a talent show, too?" Allie asked.

"Sure—the weekend after yours," Keith said.

"It's actually more of a comedy review. Which Keith is really good at—he's won before," Luke said. "So what's your act this year?"

"I'm not saying," Keith said. "I mean, that would ruin the surprise, right? And you guys want to be surprised, don't you?"

"Sure," Allie said. She gave Keith a questioning look. "But you're not planning anything that shocking, are you?"

"You never know." Keith shrugged, adjusting the packages in his arms again. "Well, great to see you, Luke—"

"Didn't you come in here to buy something?" Stephanie asked.

"Oh. Right. Actually, I just needed to stock up on gum," Keith said. "At least they still let me chew gum on probation." He moved over toward the cash register and paid for several packs of spearmint gum.

"You won't tell anyone I was talking to these guys, will you?" Luke asked Keith as he stepped up beside him.

"Hey, I don't care who you talk to," Keith said as he paid for the gum. "I'm getting so sick of all these dumb camp rules." He ripped open a pack of gum and put a piece in his mouth. He let the green wrapper fall to the floor. "Well, see you, Luke." He walked out of the store.

Stephanie frowned and picked up the wrapper.

"Steph, we'd better get a move on," Allie said. "We still have a few more stores to check out."

"No problem—I'll let you guys get back to your lipstick," Luke said. He put a hand on Stephanie's arm. "See you around?"

"I hope so," she told him.

"I'll be out sailing tomorrow—around lunch. If you can, meet me out there," Luke whispered. He leaned over and quickly kissed her cheek. Then, before Stephanie could say anything else, he was gone. She went to the front window and watched him walk down the street as Allie paid for the makeup they'd chosen.

"Why don't you just give up on Luke?" Allie asked. "He's brought you nothing but trouble."

"Give up on Luke?" Stephanie repeated. She couldn't believe how critical Allie sounded.

"Why would she do that? Stephanie and Luke make a great couple," Marguerite declared.

"Because Luke's the reason she's no longer your CIT!" Allie said. "I think you guys are blind when it comes to Luke. There's no one else who could have pulled off that vandalism at the lodge. And Sam told me Luke was the one who cut those

Stephanie laughed. "Now, that would take tal-
t. Maybe you should do another kind of dance
mber," she suggested. "One that everyone
uld participate in."

"That was my idea," Jasmine said. "But Rene
d we had to try something no one else could
."

"It only makes sense," Rene stated.

'Not if we can't do it either!" Jasmine said.
ne and Jasmine glared at each other for a
nute.

"So . . . I'll put you down for some kind of
nce," Stephanie said slowly. "And you can
rk out whatever problems you're having
ciding—"

"We're not having a problem. It's decided,"
ne said. "Swan Lake."

"Stephanie, do it with us—please?" Jasmine
ed. "Then it would be fun. I mean, you're
ng to be moving back in soon—"

Sorry." Stephanie shook her head. "I can't!"

That's okay," Rene said. "We'll do fine without
."

Rene, I don't want to interfere," Stephanie
1. "But it's really up to the cabin to choose its
Not you. I'm sort of worried—"

---

boats loose last summer! He's not a good guy.
Luke did it, Stephanie—just accept it."

"No, he didn't," Stephanie shot back. She was
shocked by how angry Allie's comments made
her. "And when I find out who really did it,
you're going to feel terrible about what you just
said!"

CHAPTER
5

◆ ◀ ◆ ◆

Stephanie glanced at her list of acts Tuesday morning. So far she had two plays, two comedy skits, one magic act, one hip-hop dance, and one cheerleading routine lined up for the talent show. What next?

"We're here."

Stephanie looked up and saw Rene standing in front of her with some campers from Brown Bear Cabin. Brown Bear was for senior campers, thirteen and fourteen years old. Stephanie had lived there her first week at camp, before she became a CIT—and she'd be moving back in on Sunday. She was dreading the move. Rene was the CIT!

"Hi, Rene," Stephanie said. She sm_____ camper with her. "Hey, Jasmine—how ___

"I'm great," Jasmine said. "Well, ac____ She glanced at Rene.

"What?" Rene asked.

"Nothing," Jasmine said. "It's just ___ we're having kind of a disagreemen___ cabin's act."

"Oh," Stephanie said. "Well, did ___ it?"

Jasmine nodded. "But—"

"Yes. And we will be doing a rend___ _Lake_," Rene announced.

"We?" Stephanie repeated as she ___ mine's expression.

"I mean—we, this cabin," Rene said___ to do ballet."

"Except that half of us have neve___ Jasmine said. "Which could be kin___ don't you think?"

"I'll teach you," Rene said. "It's ___ a problem. The better dancers w___ roles, that's all."

Jasmine put her hands on her h___ are the rest of us supposed to do? ___ our toes?"

"If I were you, I'd worry about your own act," Rene said. "Running the show!"

What's that supposed to mean? Stephanie wondered.

"Step right up! Get your tickets here!"

Stephanie smiled as she saw Cynthia, Jenny, Rene, Darah and Tiffany all standing behind a table at the camp post office the next afternoon. It was a small building located at the foot of the lake, halfway between the boys' and girls' camps. Every day at noon, mail was delivered to campers. The post office was almost always mobbed between twelve and one in the afternoon, with lines running out the door.

"Want to buy a ticket to the talent show?" Cynthia asked a group of older boys approaching the table.

Max, a waterfront CIT, wrinkled his nose. "You guys are selling tickets this year?"

He sounded so annoyed that Stephanie bit her lip. Max asked her out after Luke had been expelled from camp. Was Max still angry because she liked Luke instead of him? She thought Max was a pretty nice guy, but she didn't want to date him.

"The talent show was free last year," Sam, Allie's boyfriend, complained.

"I know. Isn't it stupid?" Darah said. She rolled her eyes.

Stephanie cleared her throat and stepped forward. "I don't think it is. Heather and Mr. McCready and the senior counselors came up with the idea. They want to make the annual talent show into a fundraiser from now on," she told Sam and Max. "The money isn't for us, or for costs or anything. We'll donate all the ticket money to a local children's charity."

"Really?" Max looked impressed. "That's a nice idea."

"I thought so, too," Stephanie said. She grinned at Max. She hoped he didn't have any hard feelings left toward her. "And maybe next year we'll get to meet some of the kids who benefited from our donation."

"How much are they going to get out of our donation? It won't be that much money," Darah said with a sneer. "Get real, Stephanie."

Max shrugged. "Don't be so sure! Anyway, every little bit helps."

"It might be enough to buy them some new toys and new clothes," Stephanie said, relieved that Max had forgiven her.

"Okay. It's definitely a good cause. How much are the tickets?" Sam asked.

"Five dollars each," Cynthia said. She glanced at Stephanie and smiled. "And it's for a good cause. Really."

"Five dollars, huh?" Sam scratched a mosquito bite on his arm. "In that case . . ." He hesitated. "Give me five tickets." Sam pulled out his wallet and took out all the money he had.

"Wow! That's so generous of you. Who are they for?" Jenny asked as Sara handed her a twenty and a five.

Sam shrugged. "Me. And anyone else who doesn't have five dollars," he told Stephanie. "Hey, have you seen Allie today?"

Stephanie nodded. She knew Allie had been hoping to see Sam. And Stephanie was hoping to see someone, too—Luke. *He said he'd be out on the lake around lunchtime today*, she remembered. *Maybe I can catch him. . . .*

More boys streamed up to the post office, including Keith. While Stephanie talked with Sam, she noticed Keith and Rene exchange angry glances.

"You've got to come," Rene was gushing to one of the Clearwater counselors. "Our acts are going to be so good. My cabin is performing a ballet!"

"That sounds like so much fun!" Keith said in a sarcastic tone. "Are you going to dress up as fairies? Or maybe ducks?" he joked. Several boys standing around the post office cracked up laughing. Keith grinned as he opened a new pack of spearmint gum and popped a piece into his mouth.

Stephanie glanced at her watch. Lunchtime was nearly over. But if she hurried, Luke might still be out on the lake.

Maybe he'll wait for me, Stephanie thought. *I don't want to miss him.*

"See you guys later," Stephanie said. "I have to run a couple of errands for the show."

"Hey!" Jenny yelled after her. "Aren't you supposed to sell tickets next?"

"Don't worry. Darcy, Kayla, and Allie will be here in a few minutes!" Stephanie called back over her shoulder.

She hurried down the path to the lake. Not too many people were hanging around, since it was lunchtime. Stephanie ran to the end of the docks and put a hand above her eyes to shield them from the sun.

She spotted a sailboat with a green, white, and blue sail tacking across the lake. It was Luke's.

Stephanie quickly pulled a canoe into the water. She grabbed a paddle and started heading toward him. *Why am I doing this?* Stephanie wondered as she struggled to make headway across the lake. Paddling a canoe alone was nearly impossible. She lifted her oar and waved it at Luke, hoping to catch his eye.

The sailboat tacked and angled toward her. *He saw me!* Stephanie thought with a thrill. She paddled a couple more strokes. The sailboat reached her a few minutes later.

"Hi!" Stephanie called to him.

"Hey! You made it after all," Luke said as a smile lit up his face. "I was about to give up on you."

He turned the boat so it was facing upwind, to keep it from moving. "It's great to see you—but aren't you supposed to be somewhere? And aren't you banned from meeting me out here for the rest of your life?"

Stephanie laughed. "Probably. But I don't care. We didn't get to talk about things the other day with everyone else around. But I wanted to tell you that I still want to prove you didn't vandalize the lodge."

"So do I," Luke said.

"Okay, then. I was wondering something. Actually, my friends and I were talking about it, and they thought someone might be framing you. So then I thought that maybe the person who tried to get you into trouble this summer is the same person who framed you last summer."

"Last summer?" Luke repeated.

"Yeah—when all the boats were cut loose. And everyone accused you," Stephanie said. "But it wasn't you—"

"Actually, Stephanie, that was me," Luke said. "I'm the one who did that."

"What?" Stephanie dropped her canoe paddle into the lake. "How could you lie to me like that?"

Luke picked up the paddle and handed it back to Stephanie. "I'm sorry. I didn't mean to lie. I just didn't think there was any point going into it—"

"Of course there was a point!" Stephanie said angrily. "You let me think you were innocent this whole time."

"And I am innocent, when it comes to whoever trashed our lodge a few weeks ago," Luke said.

"But you cut all the boats loose last year," Stephanie said. "Why would you do something like that?"

Luke sighed. "It was supposed to be a practical joke. My cabin was having this running competition to see who could get away with the best joke," he explained. "Not officially, of course—it was just a stupid idea we came up with one night when we were really bored."

Stephanie stared into Luke's eyes. "And you won? But everyone found out, and that's why you didn't get to be a CIT this year?"

"Sort of," Luke said. "I didn't confess, but word got around that I was the one who did it. Rumors fly around here—you know that."

Stephanie considered everything that Luke had just told her. She had never expected him to say he was guilty. "But it isn't a rumor. It's true."

"Yeah. But I'm through with practical jokes, Stephanie—I promise," Luke said. "I haven't done a thing this year!"

Stephanie didn't know what to think now. She was upset that Luke hadn't told her the truth. But getting into a competition of practical jokes wasn't the worst thing in the world. She couldn't get too angry about that.

Stephanie glanced back at the docks. "I should get going—the next activity starts soon."

"Okay, but hold on. Don't be mad at me, Stephanie. Please! It was a dumb stunt, but it didn't mean anything." Luke grabbed the other end of

Stephanie's canoe paddle and pulled her canoe closer to him.

Stephanie nodded. "I know."

"I'll probably fall out of the boat, but this will be worth it." He scooted out of the cockpit to the side of the boat. Then he pressed his lips against Stephanie's in a soft kiss.

The wind suddenly caught the sail and jerked the sailboat away. "Whoa!" Luke cried, as he nearly slipped off into the lake. He grabbed the edge of the cockpit with his hands and pulled himself back into it. "Bye, Stephanie!" he called as the sailboat took off.

Stephanie started paddling for shore as fast as she could. With the wind that brisk, she couldn't waste another second. *I just hope I make it back before anyone sees me—and Luke!*

CHAPTER
6

Stephanie smiled to herself as she walked into the lodge kitchen that night after dinner. She couldn't stop thinking about Luke. Every time she saw him, she felt closer to him. And when he kissed her . . .

Stephanie pushed open the swinging doors and carried the stack of dirty dessert bowls from her table over to the sink. Rene was standing on one side of the hot, steamy dishwasher. She was busy loading a tray with dirty glasses. On the other end, Tiffany was pulling out racks of clean, dry dishes. Each girl wore rubber gloves and an apron over her shorts and T-shirt, and a bandanna tied over her hair to keep it from falling into her eyes.

"How's it going?" Stephanie asked as she

placed the dirty bowls from her table on the metal surface.

"How do you think it's going?" Rene complained. "This is our third night in a row on dish duty. Thanks to you."

"Ow! Hot!" Tiffany dropped a stainless steel serving plate onto the floor. It clattered and rolled under the sink.

Three days in a row—and she still doesn't know that would be too hot to touch? Stephanie thought. She picked up the plate using a dishtowel and shoved it into the dishwasher rack so it could be washed again. "Here. Does this help?"

"Not really," Tiffany muttered.

Rene pressed a few buttons and started to send another rack of dirty dishes through the machine. "So, do you have everything ready for the talent show yet?" she asked.

Stephanie shrugged. "Not everything. The show is still a few days away. It's not ready yet, but it will be by Saturday."

"Oh, really?" Rene said. "So you're feeling pretty confident that it will go off smoothly?"

"Of course it will," Stephanie said. "Why do you ask?"

"I don't know. I was just thinking that if you

make any mistakes, or if something sort of happened to go wrong"—Rene paused—"that would really be a shame." She looked over at Tiffany and barely managed to keep from smiling. "Wouldn't it, Tiffany?"

"Oh, yeah. It would be awful." Tiffany snickered.

"Look, I know you're planning to try to ruin the talent show," Stephanie said. "It's not like you've been hiding that from anyone. But I won't let you get away with it."

"You won't be able to stop me," Rene bragged.

"What are you planning? Do you really want to ruin it for all of the campers—just to get back at me?" Stephanie asked. "How selfish can you get?"

"Me? Selfish?" Rene said. "At least you're not on probation!"

"At least you're still a CIT!" Stephanie cried.

The double doors to the kitchen swung open, and Heather walked in. "What is going on?" she demanded. "I could hear you arguing out on the porch."

Stephanie looked at Rene. "We were having a disagreement."

"Yes, I could tell. A very loud one," Heather said. "What were you arguing about?"

"Nothing," Rene said. "Nothing important."

"In that case, it'll be easy to stop. You, focus on those dirty dishes," Heather told Rene.

"That's what I was doing. Until Stephanie came in and started teasing us," Rene complained.

Heather tapped Stephanie on the shoulder. "And you, no teasing. Focus on your stage manager job, okay?"

Stephanie nodded. "I will. In fact, I'm heading to the arts and crafts shed right now to work on the sets."

"You are?" Heather asked. "Well, good. It sounds like things are going according to schedule. What types of designs are you doing?" Heather folded her arms in front of her.

"Well, I'm not completely sure, because Anna's in charge of that. She and Kayla worked on them this afternoon. Nothing fancy—bright colors and designs. We just want to make the stage look special," Stephanie explained. "Speaking of which, I'd better run—I don't want to be late. See you guys tomorrow at our next meeting!" She waved and headed for the door.

"Don't forget, Stephanie—no mistakes!" Heather called after her.

Not that she'd want to put any pressure on me or

anything! Stephanie almost laughed as she left the lodge and crossed the grassy area toward the arts and crafts building. She pulled open the door and expected to see Kayla, Anna, Darcy, and Allie all painting.

Instead they were standing with their backs to Stephanie, staring at something on the floor.

"Hey, what's up?" Stephanie greeted them. She walked in and closed the door behind her. "What are you guys looking at?" She moved toward them.

Stephanie's jaw dropped as she saw scraps of canvas and paint strewn across the floor. The flats had been torn into a hundred tiny pieces and paint spilled over them.

Stephanie felt her heart race. Rene wasn't just threatening to ruin the show. She was doing it!

CHAPTER
7

◆ ◀ ◢ ◆

"Look at this!" Stephanie said. "It's terrible." She tossed a piece of canvas into the trash can.

"Can you believe this? All the flats we painted this afternoon have been ripped up," Anna said.

Stephanie helped clean up the damaged sets. "Good thing you hadn't spent too much time on them yet," she said.

"Who would do something like this?" Allie wondered.

Anna held up a shredded piece of canvas. "It almost looks like an animal got in here."

Stephanie nodded. "Somebody got in here. But it wasn't an animal—it was a bird."

Anna stared at her. "What do you mean?"

"It was a Flamingo!" Stephanie said. "Rene hinted tonight that something could go wrong with the show. Well, she obviously followed through on her threat."

"What? Are you sure?" Kayla asked. She sounded very doubtful. "Why would she want to ruin something that she's working on, too?"

"Because she's still angry with me about her being on probation," Stephanie said. "She considers the whole thing my fault. And she knows how much is riding on this for me."

"Yeah, okay, but . . . wasn't Rene on triple kitchen duty tonight? She had to help cook, plus set the tables, plus wash the dishes. We left here right before dinner," Allie said. "So when would she have had the time to do this?"

Stephanie stared at Allie. "I can't believe you're defending Rene."

"Neither can I," Allie said. "And it doesn't come naturally, believe me. But you have to admit—she's been a little too busy to do anything but her chores," Allie said. "Never mind making more trouble for us."

"Allie's right," Darcy said. "But that doesn't mean Rene wasn't involved. She could have easily gotten someone else to do it for her. Like Cynthia, or Jenny—"

"I still don't see what they'd have to gain from ruining the sets," Anna said.

Stephanie shrugged. "Anything they do makes more work for me. And if Heather finds out . . ."

"She won't," Allie said. "We won't tell anyone. Okay?"

Stephanie nodded and everyone else agreed. "Now what?" she asked.

"We'll just have to start over and make more," Anna said. She brushed off the knees of her jeans. "No problem."

"This time, when we finish the flats, we'll hide them somewhere. Or better yet, lock them up!" Stephanie said.

"Good idea," Kayla replied. "But where? The only private places with locks are the offices in the lodge. And we'd have to ask Heather's permission, which means we'd have to tell her why we were doing it."

"I know. How about if I sleep here tonight?" Anna offered. "I have a bunch of pillows, and—"

"No. Don't be silly," Stephanie said. "We'll store everything in the lodge—backstage. Since that place is almost always full of people, nobody could get away with destroying the sets."

"Okay, everyone—start stapling new canvas across the frames," Anna said. "Then we can paint."

Later, Stephanie chose to paint a flat red with gold stars. "I'm glad we get almost all of the supplies we need from camp, or we'd be broke. Hey, speaking of money, how did the ticket sales go?"

"Great," Kayla said. "Where did you run off to?"

Stephanie smiled. She almost had a hard time believing what she'd done. "I met Luke out on the lake," she said. "I saw him out there and—"

"You did what?" Allie cried.

Stephanie was a bit taken aback by Allie's reaction, but she didn't let it show. "I talked with Luke."

"In the middle of the afternoon? When anyone could see you?" Kayla asked. She sounded almost as upset as Allie had been.

"Why do you guys have to give me such a hard time about it?" Stephanie asked. She dipped her brush into the can of red paint and started to cover the canvas flat. "You know how I feel about Luke."

"Madly, passionately, wildly in love?" Kayla teased.

Stephanie flicked a few drops of red paint at her. "No!"

"Hey!" Kayla giggled. "I look like I have the measles." She brushed at a few red dots on her arm.

"Okay, everyone—let's get to work," Anna said. "We have only an hour before lights-out."

"Hey, who's running this talent show, anyway?" Stephanie joked.

"Um . . . you are?" Anna said meekly. "And we're your humble servants, of course."

"Oh. Well, in that case . . . start painting!" Stephanie ordered.

Wednesday morning Stephanie stopped by Rene's cabin before breakfast. She wanted to catch her before the day got started. She was hoping they could talk in private. Since Stephanie had passed several of the girls from Rene's cabin on her way there, she was pretty sure she'd catch Rene alone.

Stephanie knocked on the door. "Hello?" She pushed it open slowly.

Rene poked her head out of the bathroom. Her face was covered with soapy water. "What do you want?" she asked.

"I just came by to thank you," Stephanie said.

"Thank me?" Rene rinsed her face and dabbed it dry with a towel. "For what?"

Stephanie leaned against the door frame. "For tearing apart our sets yesterday. Nice job."

Rene draped the towel on a rack and stared at Stephanie. "What sets?"

"Nice try," Stephanie said. "The sets for the talent show. They were in the arts and crafts building."

"I don't know what you're talking about," Rene said as she pulled her hair back into a clip.

"Come on. You don't have to worry, I didn't tell anyone else about it yet," Stephanie said. "The only ones who know are me, Allie, Kayla, Anna, and Darcy. And we painted new sets last night, so it's all been taken care of."

"Good," Rene said. "But why are you telling me all this?"

"Because I want you to know that as much as you try to ruin the talent show, it's not going to work," Stephanie told her. "I won't let it."

"I'm sorry about your little . . . backdrops, or whatever you call them," Rene said. "But I didn't have anything to do with it. I mean it, Stephanie."

"Funny. I don't believe you," Stephanie said.

"Well, you should," Rene told her. "Because it's someone else's fault—not mine. Maybe your boyfriend Luke had something to do with it. He likes ruining things, doesn't he?" Rene grabbed her sunglasses and sashayed out of the cabin.

Stephanie followed her down the path toward the lodge. "Luke had nothing to do with this!" she told Rene.

"Oh. Well, whatever you say."

Stephanie couldn't believe Rene was actually trying to accuse Luke of something *she'd* done. *Wait a second. This is Rene Salter. Maybe I can believe it*, she thought as they went into the lodge.

"Hey, Steph, what's up?" Darcy greeted her. She cast a curious glance at Rene. "What are you guys doing?"

"Stephanie's ranting about some sets that got damaged," Rene said. "She thinks I did it. I think Luke did it."

"Luke? But that's crazy," Darcy said. "He doesn't even live here at camp anymore."

Rene put her hands on her hips. "Show me these sets you keep talking about."

"Fine," Stephanie agreed. She, Darcy, and Rene marched back to the storeroom beside the kitchen. Stephanie and her friends had carried the sets there to be safe. *Should I show Rene where we're keeping stuff?* Stephanie wondered to herself as they opened the door.

Stephanie gasped when Darcy turned on the light. "Oh, no! Look!" Stephanie stared at the sets. Bright neon green paint had been sprayed across the flats in large swirls. "That paint," she whispered. "It's familiar. It's—"

"The same paint Luke used when he trashed the boys' lodge," Rene said smugly. "I told you it was him, not me!"

Stephanie shook her head. "It isn't Luke."

"But, Stephanie—" Darcy began.

"Maybe it's the same person who trashed the lodge. But that wasn't Luke—and this isn't either!" Stephanie declared.

CHAPTER
8

◆ ◀ ▸ ◆

"All right, crew—show me what you got!" Heather sat down at the wooden table in the center of the lodge and slapped her palm against it. The entire talent show group was meeting on Wednesday afternoon to go over everything. "Put your cards on the table, Stephanie."

Stephanie smiled uneasily. So far her "cards" included a dozen ruined flats and five Flamingoes who refused to help. But she felt she couldn't tell Heather about it—not until she figured out who was behind the vandalism. Heather would only accuse Luke if she found out about the neon green spray paint on the sets. That wouldn't help her— or Luke—at all.

Stephanie wished she could prove that the vandal was Rene. But even she had to admit that it was possible someone else was behind the sabotage. *I don't care who it is*, Stephanie thought. *I won't let anyone make me cancel the show!*

"I made a copy of the list of cabin acts and skits for you." Stephanie slid the sheet of paper across the large, round table to Heather.

Heather studied the list for a moment. "Some of these are a bit vague," she commented. "Are you sure the campers understand they have only five minutes? Did you make that clear to them?"

Stephanie nodded. "Some of the girls wanted to keep their acts secret. But I'm sure we'll find out more when we do the practice run-through tomorrow night. They'll give us their music or more information about their plans."

"Uh-huh . . ." Heather didn't sound convinced. "Well, what else do you have? How are your sets coming along?"

Stephanie bit her lip, not sure what to say.

Rene cast a superior glance her way. "I heard there might be some problems," she began.

"Well, of course there are!" Anna jumped in. "There are always problems when you don't know what you're preparing and painting for.

And then there's the fact that there are ten of us, and we can't always agree on everything," she said.

"But we're working on that!" Stephanie said. "And we'll definitely have the sets ready by rehearsal." *We'll just have to sleep with them under our beds, that's all. To keep them from getting destroyed for the third time!*

"They're practically all done now," Anna said.

"So you're in charge of sets and stage design?" Heather asked her.

Anna nodded. "Me and . . . and Jenny. Of course." She turned to Jenny with a phony smile.

Thank you, Anna! Stephanie thought.

"Jenny, what have you done so far?" Heather asked.

"Well, I signed up for sets and design." Jenny pulled her chair closer to the table. "But I've been working more on the general show concept. I've been planning the lighting scheme with Rene, and we've spoken to my dad about renting some special equipment."

What? Stephanie thought. Jenny hadn't said anything about concepts or schemes to her. But she couldn't say that now, or Heather would think she wasn't doing a good job organizing.

"We don't need special equipment," Heather said. "Do we?"

"Just a few things," Jenny said. "A strobe light, and a disco ball, and a few other things—Rene's taking care of it."

"Y—Yes," Stephanie said. "And then we have Darcy and Cynthia organizing the music. Do you guys have anything you want to tell Heather?" *Like maybe Cynthia has booked a live band to go with the lighting concept?*

Darcy and Cynthia looked across the table at each other. "We're waiting to hear from campers about what they want," Darcy said.

"I've tested the stereo system Mr. McCready said we should use," Cynthia announced. "It's working fine, so we just need to set it up. I was going to ask Darcy if she could do it after this meeting."

"Sure!" Darcy said eagerly. "Did you bring some CDs?"

Cynthia reached into her pocket and pulled out a disc. "I'm prepared." She glanced at Stephanie and smiled.

"Great. Thanks!" Stephanie told her. It figured that Cynthia was the only one of the Flamingoes really trying to help.

"Just don't play it too loud when you test it," Heather said. "And be careful. That's a very expensive system."

"We'll take good care of it," Darcy promised.

"Stephanie? What else do you have everyone working on?" Heather asked.

"Allie and Tiffany are in charge of makeup for the show," Stephanie began.

"And we'll make everyone look beautiful," Tiffany said. "Won't we, Allie? I'm even donating some from my very own private collection."

Allie rolled her eyes, and Stephanie nudged her under the table. They at least had to look like they were getting along in front of Heather.

"We don't expect any problems," Allie said. She phrased it almost like a question. She didn't sound at all convinced.

"Darah and Kayla are in charge of helping campers with their costumes," Stephanie said. "And I guess . . . that's about it."

Heather nodded. "Sounds like you have every-thing under control."

Stephanie clutched the arms of her chair. "Oh, sure. Definitely." *Unless you count the fact our sets have been trashed twice now!*

After the meeting broke up, Darcy, Cynthia,

and Jenny went off to Mr. McCready's office to get the stereo system. Rene, Tiffany, and Darah left the lodge with Heather, while Stephanie stayed behind with Allie, Kayla, and Anna.

"Can you believe them?" Anna asked. "Acting like they're actually working on the show."

Allie shrugged. "Maybe they are."

"But they're not!" Stephanie protested. "They were putting on an act for Heather."

"I don't know. They seemed sincere to me," Kayla commented. "They're working on stuff— just not with us. I got the feeling they want to put on a good show. They're even planning their own number for it, which is more than you can say for us."

"So that means only one thing," Allie concluded. "Whoever ruined the sets isn't the Flamingoes." She looked right at Stephanie. "It has to be someone else."

Stephanie didn't like what Allie was implying. Did she think Luke would try to ruin the show, when Stephanie was the person in charge of it? He wouldn't. He couldn't!

"Okay, guys, are you ready?" Stephanie called to the first act on Thursday night. Cougar Cabin

was going to run through their cheerleading routine on the lodge stage for the second time—this
time to music. Stephanie was running the rehearsal on stage, while the CITs worked with
their cabins to get the acts ready for the stage.

"Do you have our music?" one of the Cougar
campers called back. The eleven-year-old girls
were all standing in the center of the stage. When
the music started, they would fan out and take
their positions.

"Got it right here!" Stephanie called back. She
waved the disc they'd given her in the air. It was
labeled "Cougars—Do Not Steal This Disk!" She
slid it into the disc player. "Ready? Here goes!"
She pressed the Play button.

The girls shouted encouragement to one
another and waited for their music. Stephanie
stood up to watch them. Twenty seconds passed.
Forty-five seconds went by. Still no sound came
out. Stephanie knew the stereo was working—she
had helped Cynthia and Darcy test it the night
before.

"Hey, I thought you were playing our CD," a
girl called to Stephanie.

"I thought I was, too!" Stephanie said. She
crouched down and checked the stereo. The

power was on, and it looked like the CD was spinning. But no sound was coming out. She played with the volume control, but nothing happened.

"Rats!" she said. "What's wrong with this thing? Hold on, I'm going to find our music experts." Stephanie hurried to the back of the lodge, where Darcy was helping her cabin rehearse their scene. "Darcy? Could you come over here for a second?" she asked. "The stereo's not working."

"Maybe we forgot to plug it back in after we moved it," Darcy said. She followed Stephanie, and together they checked the wall outlet. "Nope. It's plugged in," Darcy said. "Hold on, I'll check the speakers."

Darcy ran to one side of the stage and stared at a blank wall. "Where are the speakers?" She reached down and picked up a frayed piece of wire. "Did somebody move the speakers?" She looked around the room and checked the left side of the stage. "This one's gone, too. I can't believe this! Somebody stole the speakers!"

CHAPTER
9

"This is unreal!" Stephanie cried. "The show is just two nights away, and we have no speakers."

"We'll have to get another stereo," Darcy said.

"I have a portable one," Cynthia offered. "It won't be as loud, but it'll work."

"That would be really great if you could go get it," Darcy said. "Thanks, Cynthia."

"You guys!" Stephanie cried. "Aren't you overlooking a major problem here? I mean, how did this even happen?"

"Who knows? The speakers might turn up tomorrow," Cynthia said. "Maybe it's just a practical joke."

"Like the fact someone tore up and painted

over our sets?" Stephanie asked. "If that's your idea of a practical joke—"

"Stephanie, Cynthia's on our side," Darcy said. "She hasn't sabotaged anything."

"I'd never ruin the talent show. None of us would," Cynthia said. "That would ruin the whole summer!"

"The point is that we need to get through this first dress rehearsal, so we can be ready for the show on Saturday night," Darcy told Stephanie. "Everything's going to be okay, Steph—just chill out a little bit."

Stephanie let out an annoyed sigh. "How am I supposed to relax when someone is deliberately messing up the show?"

"We'll take care of the music. You ask around— maybe someone heard or saw something," Darcy said. "Who knows? Maybe Heather took the speakers back. Why don't you ask her?"

Stephanie nodded. "Good idea. I'll check to see if anyone noticed anything." She started walking across the room toward Allie and Kayla.

On the way Stephanie passed Rene and the girls from Brown Bear Cabin. Rene was teaching three campers how to stand on their tiptoes. She stretched her arms over her head in a graceful movement. "Like this, Jasmine," she instructed. "And then you bend over, like so."

"Whatever," Jasmine said as she leaned down to touch her toes.

"How's *Swan Lake* going?" Stephanie asked as she stopped beside them.

"Fine," Rene said. "I designed the whole thing myself."

"Really?" Stephanie asked. "That's great." She smiled at all of the girls.

Rene put her hands on her hips. "Why? How's your stage managing going?" she asked.

"Not so good, actually," Stephanie said. "We just noticed the pair of stereo speakers are missing. You guys wouldn't happen to know anything about that, would you?"

"What's that supposed to mean?" Rene asked.

"I'm asking everyone," Stephanie said with a shrug. She looked around the circle of dancers. "Did you guys hear anything, or—"

Rene pulled Stephanie aside. "I know what you're doing."

"You do?" Stephanie asked.

"You're acting all casual, but you're trying to make it look like I took the speakers," Rene said. "You're not still obsessed with me destroying the show, are you? Because you know I'm not behind any of this."

"I don't know that," Stephanie said. "I only know the speakers are gone, and you did mention something about how it would be a shame if something went wrong with the show."

"I was joking!" Rene said. "Can't you take a joke?"

"Are you two arguing again?"

Stephanie whirled around and saw Heather standing right behind her.

"What seems to be the problem? And why is the rehearsal at a complete standstill?" Heather asked.

Stephanie couldn't hide the truth from Heather any longer. She wasn't managing the show nearly as well as she wanted to! "We just found out somebody stole the stereo speakers. So we have no music."

"What?" Heather said. "Are you sure they're stolen? Maybe they're only misplaced. Maybe a counselor borrowed them."

"Without borrowing the stereo?" Stephanie asked.

"I suppose that doesn't make much sense, does it?" Heather remarked as she tapped her chin with her index finger. "Well, do you have any idea what happened to them?"

Here goes nothing, Stephanie thought. "I have one idea," she began.

"Let's hear it," Heather said.

"I know this might sound weird, but . . . I think someone's trying to ruin the show. And maybe it's someone here, in this room. Like . . . Rene," Stephanie said.

"And I think she's completely crazy," Rene said. "I didn't steal anything, and I didn't put green spray paint on the sets the other day, and—"

"What's this about spray paint?" Heather interrupted. She looked at Stephanie. "You never told me about that! Explain," she demanded.

"We've had some problems," Stephanie said. "First we painted some flats that got slashed and cut. Then we painted some more, and those were covered with neon green spray paint—"

"Which looks just like the paint Luke Hayes used when he trashed his lodge," Rene added.

Stephanie could feel her stomach start to churn with nervousness. "Luke didn't do anything," she insisted. "Then or now! He's not even around, so it couldn't have been him. It was you, and you're trying to frame him!"

"Luke's already been kicked out of camp. So why would I want to frame him for anything?" Rene argued.

"Girls, girls! Stop it!" Heather cried. "I am really tired of your personal feud. I thought this talent show would give you an opportunity to work together and patch things up. Instead, things have gotten even worse."

Stephanie looked down at the floor. Heather was right. She did feel really badly about the whole situation. But what else was she supposed to think? "Sorry," she apologized.

"What we all need to do is get to the bottom of this," Heather declared. "Who's sabotaging the talent show? And why?"

"It's Luke," Rene said. "Isn't it obvious? His summer is ruined, so he wants to ruin ours."

"Luke doesn't care about our talent show. It's obviously someone who wants to make us think Luke did it," Stephanie said. "But it isn't Luke."

"We'll see about that," Heather said. "Until you can show me it's somebody else, Stephanie, Luke is still our prime suspect. Now, you'd better get on with your rehearsal—the show is going to happen Saturday night, no matter what."

"Don't worry. I'll find out what's going on,

even if I have to camp out here all night,"
Stephanie declared. She left Heather and Rene
and went off to find her friends. She quickly
explained everything that had just happened.

"Can you believe Rene and Heather? They both
think Luke's behind this," Stephanie said. "As if
he would be!"

Nobody said anything at first. Then Allie
cleared her throat. "I think you should start considering that Luke is the person doing all this
stuff."

"What?" Stephanie cried.

"Allie's right," Kayla said. "I just don't think
the Flamingoes would mess up something they
plan on starring in."

"Which means they wouldn't set themselves up
to look bad," Darcy agreed.

Anna rolled a pencil back and forth in her
palm. "I don't think it's the Flamingoes either."

Stephanie could hardly believe what she was
hearing. "So you all think Luke's responsible?"

Nobody said a word.

"Well, I'm sorry, but you're wrong. And I'll
prove Luke's not the one—as soon as I finish getting this talent show together!" Stephanie declared as she saw Cynthia set up her portable CD

player. She clapped her hands together and walked over to the stage. "Okay, Cougar Cabin—we've finally got the music. Now let's rehearse that routine!"

I'll have to come up with a way to catch the culprit myself, Stephanie thought. *There's no way I'm letting Luke take the blame for something he didn't do—and there's no way I'm letting anyone ruin this show! It's my one chance to show Heather and Mr. McCready I can be trusted. I'm not going to blow it!*

"This isn't the most comfortable place I've ever slept," Stephanie muttered on Friday night. She punched her makeshift pillow—a balled-up tablecloth—and stretched out on the floor of the lodge. She was lying under a window behind the door, so if anyone came in they wouldn't see her until it was too late.

Not that I know anyone's going to show up, she thought. *But I can hope. Right?*

Stephanie didn't know whether she should try to fall asleep or not. She told herself she probably ought to stay awake as long as she could. It was Friday night, and they had everything prepared for the show the next day. Stephanie had worked really hard that evening to make sure everything was ready. The show was going to be great! She knew everyone would love it, if only it could run smoothly. She wasn't about to let anyone mess with their sets, or stereo, or anything.

She ran through the order of acts in the talent show in her head. A couple of the skits were hilarious.

But after a while, Stephanie's attention drifted from the talent show to Luke. How could everyone say such awful things about him? She knew the real Luke. He'd never do the things he was accused of doing. But just because he liked to take risks sometimes, everyone thought he was dangerous.

Dangerously cute, maybe, Stephanie thought with a giggle.

Suddenly she heard footsteps on the porch outside the window. Then the door opened, nearly hitting her!

Stephanie didn't move a muscle. She'd lain down with her head facing the right direction, so she could see what was going on.

A person slowly entered the lodge. Whoever it was carried a tiny flashlight, only big enough to light up a foot or so. Stephanie's eyes adjusted to the dark and she strained to see the figure.

Sort of tall for Rene, she couldn't help thinking. But what other girl would want to ruin the show?

Stephanie crouched on her knees and reached for her flashlight. She was careful not to make any noise. She breathed quietly as she waited to see what was going to happen next. She could hear the person walking around the stage area. Then the footsteps stopped.

Stephanie heard what sounded like plastic being stacked. It's the CDs, she thought. They're taking the CDs! Stephanie couldn't wait any longer.

"Hey! Who's there?" she called out. "What are you doing?"

There was a loud clatter as whoever it was dropped all of the CDs. They crashed against the wood floor, and Stephanie heard the plastic cases crack.

"Oh, no!" a boy's voice said.

Stephanie froze as she heard him running for the door. *It's a guy?*

CHAPTER
10

◆   ◄   ▪   ◆

Stephanie's finger was on the flashlight button, but she was too stunned to press it and turn it on. Finally, just as the boy was running out the door, Stephanie managed to click the button.

She had the flashlight pointed at his feet. All she could see was a pair of white tennis sneakers with a blue stripe on them. She leapt to her feet and tried to follow. The boy disappeared into the woods on a path leading back to Camp Clearwater.

Stephanie started to chase him. She shined the flashlight ahead of her, but she couldn't see anything except what looked like a big white circle disappearing into the trees.

Stephanie bumped into a branch that poked her in the eye. "Who are you?" she called out. "Why are you doing this?"

Stephanie couldn't ask the question she really wanted to. But all she could think was:

What if that was Luke?

I'd know his voice, she told herself. *That wasn't him.*

Without having seen his face, though, she couldn't be a hundred percent sure. What other boy would it be?

Stephanie walked back into the lodge and turned on the overhead light. She started to pick up the cracked CD cases and put the CDs back. She looked all around for a clue, to see if the thief had left any more evidence behind. White tennis shoes with a blue stripe . . . It wasn't much to go on.

Stephanie closed her eyes and tried to picture Luke wearing sneakers. She knew he had orange suede skateboarding sneakers—she'd seen him in those. But mostly he wore sandals. Half the times she'd seen him, he was barefoot!

Now what? Stephanie thought. *Do I search Camp Clearwater and question every boy with white tennis shoes with a blue stripe?*

* * *

Right after finishing her morning chores on Saturday, Stephanie stopped by the soccer field to see Darcy.

Darcy was running a soccer game—a young girls' team against a young boys' team. On the other side of the field, Keith and Max were coaching the boys' team. Darcy wore red nylon soccer shorts and a long T-shirt. A whistle hung on a lanyard around her neck.

Stephanie waved as she walked up to her friend. "Hi, Darcy."

Darcy looked over at Stephanie. "Hey! What are you doing here? Don't you have a billion last-minute errands to run?"

Stephanie pushed strands of damp hair out of her face. "I've been running around like crazy getting everything ready for tonight!" She walked up to Darcy and stood beside her. "But I came by because I really need to talk to you," she said. "Do you have a minute, or are you too busy?"

"I can talk," Darcy said. "Until someone scores a goal or commits a foul. What's up?"

"You were right. I really did have the wrong idea about Rene and the Flamingoes ruining the show. I mean . . . well, I have some news. And it's kind of . . . serious news."

Darcy turned to her. "What? Stephanie, you're worrying me!"

"Don't worry—just help me figure out what to do. I camped out last night on the lodge floor," Stephanie explained. "Somebody came in and tried to take all the CDs for the talent show."

"What? You're kidding!" Darcy grabbed Stephanie's wrist. "So did you catch the person? Who is it?"

Stephanie frowned as she shook her head. "I didn't catch anyone. But I did say something, and whoever it was got scared and dropped all the CDs. Most of the cases are broken, but the discs seem fine. I spent most of the night testing them. I cleaned up the mess, and I—I didn't sleep at all—"

Darcy's eyes widened. "Did you tell Heather what happened? Wait—who was it? You never said."

"No, I didn't tell Heather. And I don't know who it was," Stephanie said. "I didn't want to tell her. I haven't told anyone—except you."

Darcy let go of Stephanie. "Why me?"

"Because I might need your help," Stephanie said. She glanced at the soccer game and then looked at Darcy. "I found out that whoever is trying to wreck the talent show isn't a Flamingo—for sure. I mean, he might have been put up to it by the Flamingoes, but—"

"He?" Darcy nearly shrieked.

Stephanie nodded. "The person I caught last night was a guy. But I didn't get a good look at him. I only saw his sneakers, because I got so freaked out, I couldn't get my flashlight on soon enough. Then he took off for the boys' camp."

Darcy kicked at a twig on the ground. "Man! I can't believe this!" She shook her head. "Don't get mad at me again, Steph, but I have to ask this. Do you think it was Luke?"

Stephanie stared across the field at Keith. He was racing after a ball that had gone out of bounds. Stephanie noticed the white sneakers on his feet and thought back to the night before when she'd fumbled with her flashlight. Why hadn't she been able to see anything?

Then she glanced at Max, yelling instructions to some of the boys. He had on white sneakers, too.

Darcy waved her hand in front of Stephanie's face. "Stephanie? Do you?"

Stephanie blinked. "Do I what?"

"Do you think it was Luke?" Darcy asked.

"No, I don't. The voice didn't sound like his— but I can't be a hundred percent sure. Do you have any other ideas?" Stephanie asked. "I mean, it has to be someone who likes making trouble. And they'd have to have something against me— which Luke doesn't."

Darcy stared at her. "I can think of someone who's pretty mad at you right now." She gestured across the field toward Keith. "He thinks you're the reason he's on probation."

Stephanie shrugged. "Yeah. He was pretty rude when Allie and I saw him in town on Monday. But wouldn't he be more mad at Rene than me?"

Darcy snapped her fingers. "He might not know you're in charge. Maybe he only wants to ruin Rene's act!"

Stephanie thought back to the day in the post office when Rene had been talking about her special performances. Keith had really given her a hard time. "He definitely might do something to make her look bad."

"They were selling the tickets when he was there," Darcy said. "Maybe he thinks they're running the show. He can get back at Rene and Tiffany at the same time!"

"Exactly!" Stephanie said. "I wish I'd thought of that before. How can we find out if it's him?"

"We can't just accuse him." Darcy gave Stephanie a knowing look. "That never works."

"He'll deny everything, and we have no proof," Stephanie agreed. "And now that he knows we might be on to him, he might even quit trying to sabotage the show."

"I don't know. Whoever it is, he's done a lot to ruin it so far," Darcy said. "Why stop now?"

"You have a point," Stephanie said. "So what should we do?"

"I guess we'll have to watch him really carefully during the show tonight," Darcy said. "If it's him, we'll find out."

"And if it isn't . . . whoever it is will get away with ruining the show," Stephanie said. "Let's go talk to him. I did hear the guy's voice last night. Maybe I can tell if it was Keith for sure."

"No problem." Darcy put the whistle around her neck in her mouth and blew hard on it. "Okay, guys! Time!" she yelled.

"Aw . . ." Most of the players groaned, disappointed the game was over.

"Time for a break, that's all!" Darcy called to them. "Take five, have some water, and be ready for the second half." She and Stephanie jogged across the field to Keith. Max waved at them and

hurried toward the bench to give the soccer players some water.

"Why'd you stop the game?" Keith asked. He
was dribbling a soccer ball.

Stephanie tried to remember the voice she'd
heard last night. It all happened so fast, and he'd
only said, "Oh, no."

"The kids looked like they needed a break. And
I wanted to ask you something," Darcy said.

"What are you doing here?" Keith asked
Stephanie.

"I came by to go over some last-minute stuff
with Darcy," Stephanie said. "For the talent show
tonight. You are coming, aren't you?"

Keith's feet got caught up, and he nearly tripped
over the ball. "Whoa. I really need to practice more.
Yeah, I'm coming. Of course. So what did you want
to ask me?"

"Um . . . you know that thing at the lake this
afternoon?" Darcy asked. "What time is that? And
how does it work again?"

Stephanie admired the way Darcy was getting
Keith to talk. But his voice wasn't distinctive
enough. Stephanie couldn't tell whether he was
the one she'd heard the night before.

"What's going on at the lake?" Stephanie asked. "I didn't hear about anything."

"How could you? You've been too busy," Darcy said.

"A few senior campers from both camps are going to try to swim all the way across the lake," Keith explained. "They act like it's a big deal, but it's not that hard. Luke and I did it one afternoon a couple of years ago—the same weekend as the Midnight Moonlight Sail."

The Midnight Sail! Stephanie felt her heart start beating faster. *That's it—the big white circle I saw before. It was on Keith's Moonlight Sail T-shirt!*

Luke said he had the same T-shirt, but it had fallen apart the summer before. How many other campers had that shirt? Max had one, she remembered. And who else? Didn't they say it was only the best sailors who got to do it?

"All the CITs and counselors are going to be down at the lake," Keith went on. "We're supposed to cheer the swimmers on and row support boats. It'll be fun." He glanced over at Max and the campers, who had started their game without him or Darcy. "Hey, wait up!" he called as he ran over to them.

"Well?" Darcy asked. "Get anything?"

"Maybe," Stephanie said. "But it's not enough."

"I know," Darcy said. "You could go check out some of the boys' cabins while we're down at the lake this afternoon. Including Keith's, of course."

"Do you really think I'll find anything?" Stephanie asked.

"You might," Darcy said. "If he has this incredible stereo system in his cabin, then it might be him."

Stephanie laughed. "I'll do it. Just make sure he doesn't leave the lake."

"I'll do even better. I'll make sure he's in my canoe," Darcy said. "He won't get back to shore without me!"

"But . . . won't that be weird?" Stephanie asked. "I mean, you guys went out that one time—"

"Oh, please. Anything for friendship!" Darcy said.

Stephanie picked her way carefully along the path up to the cabins late on Saturday afternoon. So far she hadn't bumped into anyone. That was exactly the way she wanted it. She had seen a few boys when she first got to Clearwater, and she told them she came over to borrow supplies for the talent show. Then she confirmed with them that she was headed to the right cabins.

This is my last day to get everything ready for the show, she thought. *Instead I'm spending the whole day trying to catch the person who's trying to ruin the show!*

Stephanie stopped at Max's cabin first. She slowly opened the door. "Hello?" She walked in and turned on the light.

She looked around the cabin for Max's bunk. Nothing was labeled, and she didn't know him well enough to recognize his stuff. She checked out everyone's metal camp trunk. She noticed the label on the end of the first trunk. It was Max's.

Stephanie was so nervous that she fumbled with the latch a few times. Finally she pulled the lid up.

She searched through the trunk, but found nothing but clean T-shirts, socks, shorts, and a few books. Nothing that would link Max to the sabotage.

I guess Max isn't the culprit, Stephanie decided as she quickly closed the trunk and slipped out of the cabin. *Now on to Keith's cabin.*

She crept through the woods until she reached Keith's cabin. No one was around, and once again she sneaked inside.

Stephanie quickly checked the trunk labels until she found Keith's name. With trembling fingers she undid the latch and opened the lid.

Sitting on top of a jumbled mess of tennis rackets and bats and balls was a pair of white sneakers with a blue stripe on them. "Aha!" Stephanie said. She grabbed one of the sneakers and pulled it out into the light. Dots of neon green paint were splattered on the toe.

If these are Keith's, she thought, *then he sprayed the sets the other night. Or he could have worn them way back when he trashed the boys' lodge. But is this enough evidence?*

Stephanie heaved a sigh and leaned back against the bunk bed. As she did, she felt something against her back. She turned around and saw something bulky covered by a sleeping bag.

She felt really strange going through someone else's things. But she couldn't resist. She pulled off the sleeping bag.

Two black stereo speakers were lying underneath, covered by clothes!

CHAPTER

11

◆ ◀   ◾   ◆

"Luke? I think I know who framed you," Stephanie said as soon as Luke answered the telephone Saturday night.

It was only half an hour before the talent show was supposed to start. *I can't believe I haven't had a chance to call him before now,* Stephanie thought. She had sneaked back upstairs to use the phone in Heather's office after getting everything set up onstage. Heather had given Stephanie a key so that she could use her office to store the stereo system and all the CDs.

"Stephanie? Doesn't the talent show start soon?" Luke asked.

"Yes—and I'm sorry I didn't call sooner," Stephanie said. "It's been so hectic, and I've been dying to talk to you. I haven't even told anyone but Darcy about this yet." She'd found Darcy a few minutes earlier and explained what she found in Keith's cabin.

"What are you talking about?" Luke asked. "I mean, how do you know for sure that someone framed me? What happened?"

Stephanie quickly explained the talent show sabotage. Then she told Luke what had happened the night before, and how she had seen Keith's T-shirt, and found neon green paint splattered on the sneakers in his trunk. "Maybe it wouldn't hold up in court or anything, but I think we have a case—"

"Keith? He had something to do with this?" Luke interrupted. He sounded stunned. "But we were friends—I thought we were, anyway."

"I'm sorry, Luke, but it really looks like Keith's the one who did all this," Stephanie said. She didn't hear a response. "Luke? Are you okay?"

"I'm so mad right now, I can't even think straight," Luke said. "Keith had the nerve to get me kicked out of camp? And he's hanging around pulling more practical jokes while I'm the one who's sitting at home all summer?"

"I know—it's awful!" Stephanie agreed. "That's why I'm calling you. I need you to come to the talent show and watch Keith. I think he's going to try something tonight."

"So just tell Mr. Davis—and Mr. McCready and Heather," Luke said. "I'll call them right now—they won't hate me anymore, and you can be a CIT again—"

"No!" Stephanie interrupted. "We can't just accuse Keith. We need to have proof."

Luke let out a frustrated sigh. "And how are we supposed to get proof?"

"I don't know. But I do know he's been trying to sabotage the talent show all week. I don't know whether it's to get back at me, or to ruin it for Rene." Stephanie told Luke about all the things that had happened since she saw him on the lake that day.

"You know what? I bet he wasn't buying stuff for his comedy act when we saw him at the drugstore that afternoon," Luke said. "He must have been buying the spray paint and other stuff he needed. That's why he didn't want us to see into the bags."

"I forgot about that," Stephanie said. "Now that makes me feel even more nervous. Because I can't help thinking he'll try to pull something else," Stephanie said. "Tonight."

"Look at it this way. If he does, and we catch him, we'll have proof," Luke said. "They won't be able to argue with that."

"If we catch him?" Stephanie asked. "How can we do that?"

"The show starts in twenty-five minutes, right? I'll be there," Luke said.

"I know I asked you to come, Luke. And I want you to be here—but be super careful. If you get caught . . ." Stephanie didn't finish the sentence.

"The only one who's going to get caught is Keith," Luke said with determination. "I'll wear a baseball cap and sneak in during the middle of someone's act. No one will even notice me—I promise."

"How are you going to get here that fast?" Stephanie asked.

"I'll come by boat," Luke said.

There was a rumble of rolling thunder outside. "Did you hear that?" Stephanie asked. "You shouldn't be out on the lake tonight! Anyway, it's already dark."

"I'll ride my bike, then," Luke said. "Good luck, Stephanie, and I'll see you soon."

"Bye, Luke," Stephanie said just as he hung up on his end of the line. "Can't wait to see you," she mumbled as she replaced the receiver.

"Aha!" Rene said as she strode into the open doorway. "So you are still talking to Luke—and on Heather's phone? You've got a lot of nerve, Stephanie."

"T-talking to whom?" Stephanie asked as she busied herself stacking CDs.

"Luke, who else?" Rene said. "I came up to see what was taking you so long. We're starting soon, you know."

Stephanie felt badly about having accused Rene of sabotaging the show. *Maybe I should confide in her*, she thought. *Maybe she can help me catch Keith, too.*

"But instead of being the stage manager, like you're supposed to be, you're up here talking to Luke," Rene said. "That figures. Have you noticed that there's a raging thunderstorm about to start? I hope the roof doesn't leak." She gazed up at the ceiling. "So why were you calling Luke now?"

Stephanie finished collecting the last few CDs and headed for the door. There was so much to do—she didn't have time to explain everything and apologize to Rene just then. "I'm sorry, Rene.

I've got to run downstairs," she said. "But I promise I'll tell you all about it later."

The chairs in the lodge were almost full with boys from Clearwater. The judges were seated at a folding table to the right just below the stage. Heather was explaining the judging system to Mr. McCready and to Tracey, the head counselor from Loon Cabin.

Heather tapped her wristwatch. "Fifteen minutes until curtain," she called to Stephanie.

So much for starting late, Stephanie thought. With Heather around, that wouldn't be possible. She smiled weakly at Heather and gave her the thumbs-up signal.

Campers were running around doing last-minute rehearsals and looking nervous and excited. Stephanie could hear singing in the kitchen, and one group was rehearsing their play in the large coat closet, with the door closed.

Darcy came up to Stephanie and took the CDs from her arms. "Stephanie, is everything okay?" she asked.

Stephanie shrugged. "I just talked to Luke, and he's coming here so he can watch Keith during the show. I'm still worried Keith is going to try to ruin the show."

"Stephanie, you've got to come backstage," Allie said, rushing up to both of them. "Darcy, you, too."

"What's wrong?" Stephanie asked.

"There's something you have to see," Allie said.

They raced to the makeshift backstage area. Partition walls created a private area between the back of the stage and the kitchen. Inside the walls were tables where people could sit and apply makeup. There were also racks for clothes and a table with a couple of pitchers of water and plastic cups set out.

Allie led Stephanie and Darcy to the center table, with the largest mirror.

There was a white sheet of paper taped to the mirror. On it someone had written in black felt-tip pen: "It'll Take All Your Talent to Pull This Off Tonight! Good Luck, Break a Leg, and Don't Be Afraid of the Dark!"

"What's that supposed to mean?" Allie asked. "And who do you think wrote it?"

Stephanie spotted a green piece of paper on the floor. She crouched down and picked up a spearmint-gum wrapper. *Keith left his trademark calling card,* she thought.

Darcy leaned closer to Stephanie. "That looks

like Keith's handwriting," she said. "I've seen signs he made for our soccer games."

Out onstage Stephanie heard Heather tell the audience to take their seats. There was less than a minute to showtime.

"Don't be afraid of the dark . . ." Stephanie repeated slowly. "I don't know what it means—but it gives me the creeps!"

Hurry, Luke, she thought.

CHAPTER
12

♦ ◂ ◆ ♦

"Welcome to Camp Sail-Away's twenty-third annual talent show!" Stephanie threw open her arms.

The audience cheered, and Stephanie could hear all the girls waiting offstage applauding as well. She glanced down from the stage at Mr. McCready and Heather. They were both smiling up at her. Heather was holding a pen and a notebook. *She's probably ready to write down all the mistakes I make*, Stephanie thought.

Stephanie adjusted the sleeves of her black tuxedo jacket and smiled out at the crowd. Her hair was pulled back with a black and white ribbon, and she wore a white T-shirt and a short black miniskirt.

"Before we get started, I'd really like to thank everyone who helped with this year's show." *Which would be everyone here except Keith*, she thought as she glanced around the audience. Keith was sitting with Tyler and some of his other buddies in the very last row of seats. She didn't see Luke, but she didn't expect to—not yet.

Before Stephanie could go on with her thank-yous, there was a loud rumble of thunder.

"Well, it sounds like we're in for a very exciting night!" Stephanie joked. "I know we have lots of great acts lined up, and now the weather's joining in. It's a good night to be inside. But back to my thanks. I want to acknowledge all of the CITs— each and every one contributed to the show, and I really appreciated the help. And I also want to thank Heather for all of her organizing genius." Stephanie bowed to Heather. *It's never too late to score a few points*, she thought. Heather's face even turned a little pink from the compliment.

"Now, if you all look at your programs, you'll see the acts we have planned for you tonight." Heather had let Stephanie type up a program on her computer. Kayla copied it, and Tiffany handed them out earlier that night. "We'll have a brief intermission halfway through. So—"

There was another loud crack of thunder. Stephanie glanced at the windows and then smiled nervously at the crowd. "I'm sure you're as eager to see the first act as I am. So, without any further ado, I give you . . . Dolphin Cabin with their own interpretation of Snow White and the . . . Nine Dwarfs!"

Stephanie hustled off stage as Darcy and Cynthia started the music. Rene hit the lights to set the scene, while Anna made a last-minute adjustment to the cot onstage.

The Dolphins were Allie's cabin. Stephanie smiled as nine eight-year-old campers marched single file on to the stage, singing, "We are the dwarfes! We are the dwarfs!" Each girl wore a T-shirt with her dwarf name painted on it. The two extra dwarfs were named "Cranky" and "Spanky." Cranky tripped the others until they all tumbled to the ground like bowling pins. Then Spanky waved a paddle made of foam rubber and spanked them all with it! The audience howled with laughter.

Another eight-year-old girl, the tallest, stepped onstage dressed as Snow White in a white night-gown. Allie, playing the wicked stepmother, followed her, wearing a T-shirt that said "Evil" in large hand-painted letters. She was carrying a red apple, which she handed to the girl in the night-gown. Snow White bit into the apple and collapsed onto the cot. All the dwarfs cried except Spanky, who chased the wicked stepmother and spanked her off the stage. Then Sam, Allie's boyfriend, made a surprise entrance to kiss Snow White. But the dwarfs wouldn't let him near her! They tackled him, and Spanky spanked him, too! When Snow White sat up, startled by the commotion, Spanky swatted her with his paddle until she jumped up and ran off the stage. Sam followed, with all the dwarfs chasing after him.

The audience burst into applause. Just as Stephanie went onstage to introduce the next act, lightning flashed through the windows. Then a piercing crack of thunder split the air outside. Rene dimmed the overhead lights for the next act and more lightning illuminated the hall. Strange shadows flickered across the stage as the room went pitch-black in preparation for Cougar Cabin's cheerleading routine. *I hope Luke's going to be okay*, Stephanie thought as she heard rain lash against the windowpanes. *He probably got caught outside right in the middle of this storm!*

When music blasted out of the stereo, Stephanie nearly jumped. The girls on stage wore matching black T-shirts with dozens of glued-on sequins that reflected the swirling bright lights Rene was shining on them. Firecracker sounds kicked off the opening sequences, as the girls did kicks, jumps, and flips. Stephanie couldn't believe how coordinated the team had gotten in just one week. *They'll get a prize for sure,* she thought.

As she stepped up to introduce the next few acts, Stephanie gazed into the crowd. She wanted to know where Keith was at all times. But each time she checked, he was sitting in his seat. He hadn't budged.

So far so good, Stephanie thought as she watched Anna's cabin of seven-year-old campers perform a cute dance number. *Everything is going great!*

"And now," Stephanie said, amazed by how quickly the show was going, "we're up to our fifth act." She glanced behind her at Jasmine and the rest of the girls from Brown Bear Cabin. She wouldn't want to be in their shoes—for anything! *Good thing I'm not moving back in there until tomorrow,* she thought with a chuckle.

"Ladies and gentlemen . . ." Stephanie said as Darcy played a tape of a drum roll. "I'm very pleased to present Brown Bear Cabin to you— doing a dance from Swan Lake!"

Stephanie stepped off to the side of the stage. Rene crouched nearby as she helped everyone assume their correct ballet positions. She had arranged for Darah to operate the lights since she needed to be closer to the action.

Stephanie tried not to snicker as the music began and the girls all moved in different directions. Then a few of them tried to stand on their toes. They wobbled and tilted as they grimaced in pain. Two of them simply gave up and ran back and forth across the stage, leaping in time to the music.

Stephanie watched Rene carefully. Her jaw was clenched, as if she were gritting her teeth, and her forehead was creased with worry. Stephanie knew this horrible performance had to be killing her. Rene couldn't tolerate coming in last—in anything. But if her cabin's act kept up this way, that was exactly what would happen.

Half of the dancers held a dramatic position with their arms gracefully extended above their heads. But the other half flung their arms out and hit each other in the face!

Suddenly there was a white flash of lightning and a gigantic crack of thunder. The vibrations nearly shook the walls of the building, and the CD skipped.

Stephanie glanced out the window behind her. The storm was getting more intense by the minute. She counted the seconds between the thunder and the next flash of lightning. One second. The storm center was less than a mile away!

The campers lost track of their places and glanced at Rene for help. But it was hard to hear the music with the rumbling and crackling.

There was one last zigzag of lightning and then all of the lights in the lodge went out. The entire place was thrown into darkness!

CHAPTER
13

◆ ◀ ◆ ◆

Campers started screaming and shouting. Some were joking around, but many were truly scared. Stephanie reached for the wall behind her as her eyes slowly adjusted to the darkness. All around her, kids were yelling.

"Let's see if all the lights at camp went out!"

"Talk about a storm!"

"Check out that lightning!"

"I can't even see my hands!"

Stephanie caught a brief glimpse of the lodge in a flash of lightning—it was complete chaos! Everyone was crowded around the windows. Her mouth opened wide as a giant bolt of lightning struck the top of a tall pine tree just yards away from the lodge's front door.

"Okay, everyone—settle down! It's all right!" Stephanie assured the crowd. "I told you it would be an exciting show, and it is—right?"

"What are we going to do?" a girl's voice cried out.

"Let's go back to Clearwater!" a couple of the guys were saying. "I bet we have electricity."

Stephanie heard Marguerite's voice just behind the stage and slowly moved toward it. "Marguerite! Are you okay?" Stephanie called. She tried to see the back of the lodge, where Keith had been sitting. *Was Keith still there?* she wondered. *Had Luke arrived yet?*

"Stephanie!" Marguerite cried, grabbing Stephanie's hand. "I'm okay. But this is pretty weird! Is this part of some Camp Sail-Away tradition?"

"No way," Stephanie said.

Heather finally made her way on to the stage. "Please, everyone! Stay calm!" she cried. "Don't be afraid of the dark!"

"Heather sounds totally scared," Marguerite commented.

"Oh, no. She's just excited," Stephanie told her. *I can't believe it. Keith wrote that note. He knew this storm was coming. But this isn't the storm at all—he planned this!*

But how am I going to catch him? Or is Luke here doing that already?

"How can Heather be excited at a time like this?" Marguerite asked.

"Oh, you know Heather—she probably wants to get everything fixed right away, that's all," Stephanie said.

Mr. McCready turned on another flashlight and finally joined Heather on the stage. "We have flashlights and everything's fine!" he called in a booming voice. There's a generator downstairs that should kick in soon, but . . . never mind, there's nothing to worry about even if it doesn't. It's just a thunderstorm," Mr. McCready said. "And, as we all know, storms pass. This one will be gone in ten minutes," he predicted.

"I'll call the power company to find out what's going on, and Mr. McCready will check the lines outside," Heather told the hushed crowd. "They'll get the power back on—probably before we even call them!"

"In the meantime, counselors, help your campers find their seats again," Mr. McCready said. "Stephanie? You know what your job is."

"Yes?" Stephanie asked.

"Keep these people entertained!" Mr. McCready said. "The counselors will help you keep the campers in their seats, but you have to entertain them."

"But how?" Stephanie asked as Mr. McCready was leaving.

Heather pulled her closer. "Do whatever you have to—just keep them entertained until we get back. I'm going to the office to call and Mr. McCready will be outside checking the lines." The last thing we need is a hundred panicky campers!"

"They're not panicking," Stephanie said.

"Good. And they won't, as long as they have something fun to focus on while we get the power back on. See you as soon as we can!" She hurried out after Mr. McCready.

"Okay, Stephanie." Rene walked up on stage next to her. Darah, Cynthia, Jenny, and Tiffany all followed. "What do we do now?"

"What a complete disaster," Jenny said. "I can't believe the generator didn't go on!"

"Yeah, and it had to happen right in the middle of my act!" Rene said. "Talk about lousy timing. We were just getting to my solo."

Jenny put a hand over her mouth to stifle a laugh.

Rene glared at her.

"Sorry," Jenny said with another snicker. "Whoops! I didn't mean that you were sorry, I meant, you know, I was. About your act."

But as soon as she controlled her giggles, Darah and Tiffany started laughing. Then Cynthia let out a laugh. When Darcy and Kayla came up onto the stage, Darcy asked, "What's so funny?"

"We were talking about Rene's *Swan Lake* dance," Jenny said. "How it was going when the power went out."

Darcy snickered. "You couldn't have wished for a better time to lose power," she said.

"You know what?" Rene began in an angry tone. Then she stopped and started laughing. "You're right!"

By the time Allie and Anna joined the group, everyone was in hysterics—Rene included.

"I guess this is what they mean by nervous energy," Stephanie said. "Because that's the only way to explain our getting along this well with the Flamingoes! Sorry, Rene."

"It's okay," Rene said. "Maybe we should have planned to do a comedy act."

"Don't sweat it—you might win for best comedy anyway," Darah told her.

"Okay, you guys. Time to get serious," Stephanie said. "Heather and Mr. McCready asked us to entertain the troops, so that's what we're going to do."

"Are you trying to be funny?" Jenny asked. "I mean, how do you expect people to go on? No one can see the stage."

"Jenny's right," Allie said.

Stephanie concentrated for a second. "How about a sing-along? We don't need lights in order to sing."

"I'll lead it," Rene offered. "I know lots of great camp songs."

"Perfect!" Stephanie said.

"Cynthia and Darcy? Go to the kitchen and see if you can find some more flashlights," Stephanie instructed. "And maybe some candles."

"Aye aye, Skipper," Darcy joked. She and Cynthia headed carefully toward the kitchen.

"Anna and Jenny? You were doing sets." Stephanie scratched her head.

"We could set the mood," Anna suggested. "We could go into the audience and get everyone kind of joking around so people forget that it's sort of scary being here with no lights."

"Great idea!" Jenny said. "You know what? My dad has a giant stash of candy in his office. Why don't we go get it and we can hand it out while we wait for the sing-along to start?"

"Brilliant," Anna told her. They linked arms and started feeling their way toward the stairs.

"Darah and Kayla, how about if you help Anna and Jenny with crowd control?"

"I'd love to," Kayla said.

Darcy and Cynthia came back a few minutes later carrying half a dozen flashlights and one lit candle.

"Is that all you could find?" Stephanie asked, disappointed.

"We bumped into Jenny on the way, and she said there are some more candles in the basement and maybe some kerosene lamps," Rene said. "We really need more light than this, or people might fall down."

"I'll go down to the basement," Stephanie said. "Could you get these flashlights spread out around the audience so people can see where they are?" She pointed to the tall red candle. "Could I borrow that?"

"You're sure you don't want me to go to the basement with you?" Rene offered.

"No—but thanks," Stephanie said. She was genuinely touched by Rene's offer. It's not often the Flamingoes wanted to help. Actually, *it's never happened before*, Stephanie thought as she cupped her hand around the burning flame to keep it from going out. But right now Stephanie wanted to do some looking around on her own. She'd completely lost track of Keith—and she didn't know if Luke had even made it.

"I'll see you guys in a minute!" Stephanie took the steps down to the basement slowly. She could hear the thunder moving farther away as the storm's intensity decreased. *What was it that Mr. McCready said about a backup generator?* she wondered as her foot hit the bottom step.

Stephanie stood at the bottom of the steps and held the candle out in front of her so she could see where she needed to go. There was a door marked "Linens" and one had a sign that said "Janitorial Supplies." Which one would have candles?

Stephanie started down the hallway and saw there was a third room. She stepped forward.

A tall figure moved in the darkness, and Stephanie gasped in surprise. "Who—who is it?" she stammered.

"Who are *you*?" the figure replied.

CHAPTER
14

◆ ◀ ◣ ◆

"Luke! It's me," Stephanie said as the candle lit up the small supply room. "You made it." She set the candle on a shelf and threw her arms around Luke.

"Shh! Quiet," Luke warned. "Besides, you might be sorry you did that," he said as he hugged Stephanie.

"Why's that?" Stephanie asked. As she stepped back, she realized her tuxedo jacket was now completely soaked from the rainwater on Luke's nylon windbreaker. His hair was dripping wet, and his blue jeans were drenched with water and mud.

"I know—I get zero points for neatness," Luke said as he slicked his hair back.

"That's okay," Stephanie said. "This isn't exactly a night where everything's going perfectly. So what are you doing down here?"

"I got here right before the lights went out," Luke whispered. "I had just enough time to spot Keith—and watch him take off right before the blackout!"

Stephanie's eyes widened. "I knew he did it!"

Luke put a finger on Stephanie's lips. "Shh! He's down here somewhere."

"He is?" Stephanie mouthed.

Luke nodded. "I followed him. Wait—did you just hear something?"

Stephanie didn't move. She heard footsteps at the other end of the hall. "Someone is down there," she whispered.

"That's where all the fuses are," Luke said. "Maybe it's Keith! Let's check it out." He started moving down the hallway.

Stephanie grabbed his coat sleeve. "What if it's Mr. McCready trying to fix the power?" she asked. "We'll be in so much trouble!"

"You go first," Luke told her. "If the coast is clear, then I'll come out. Deal?"

Stephanie nodded. She moved slowly and carefully toward the end of the hall. She held the candle in front of her with one hand and crossed her fingers behind her back with the other.

Suddenly someone stepped out of the shadows, and Stephanie nearly tripped over his feet.

"Keith!" she said out loud.

"Oh, um, hi, Stephanie," Keith said as she shone the candle in his face. "What are you doing down here?"

"Getting extra candles," Stephanie said.

Luke stepped out from the supply room. "And wondering why the emergency power didn't kick right in. Which is something you probably know all about."

"What?" Keith scoffed. "Where did you come from?"

"I came to watch the show. But then I saw you turn off the power," Luke bluffed. "And then you disabled the generator."

"I don't know what you're talking about. I came down here looking for candles," Keith said. "Is that a crime?"

"Then why did you pass right by the supply closet? What are you doing here by the fuse boxes?" Luke demanded.

"It's dark! I got lost," Keith said.

"You're carrying a flashlight," Stephanie pointed

out. "How could you get lost? Are you really down here to turn off all the lights? You left that note on the mirror, didn't you—the one that said not to be afraid of the dark. And then you turned off the lights in the middle of Rene's act—right when all the kids were scared by the thunderstorm!"

"I didn't turn off anything," Keith said. "I wouldn't even know how!"

"Yes, you would," Luke said with a confident grin. "Don't you remember? We learned how once. Mr. Davis gave us that special training last year. What to do in case of emergency." He shook his head. "Trust you to turn it into a big practical joke at the annual talent show. Well, you got everyone pretty good."

"What do you mean?" Keith narrowed his eyes.

"People were scared half to death! Weren't they, Stephanie?" Luke asked. "You couldn't have planned it any better. Hold on—don't tell me. Was this your act for next weekend's talent show?"

Keith smiled. "The storm was a nice touch, wasn't it? I didn't even know it was coming. And it's cool, because it's the perfect alibi."

"Except for one thing," Stephanie said.

"What?" Keith asked.

"The fact that you left a bunch of clues behind," Stephanie said. "Not tonight—but the other times."

"What other times?" Keith said. He turned to Luke. "What's she talking about?"

"I think I have a pretty good idea," Luke said, his voice starting to pulse with anger. "Like, for instance, I know you have that paint on your shoes right now because you vandalized the lodge and made everyone think it was me. And you sprayed that paint all over the sets for this talent show and tried to make people think I did it." He took a few steps toward Keith and looked even angrier.

Keith didn't say anything for a minute. "Well, hey," he said. "You have to admit it was a pretty good practical joke."

Luke narrowed his eyes. "Which part?"

"The part where you got kicked out of camp instead of me," Keith said.

"So you confess?" Stephanie asked.

Keith shrugged. "Sure. What difference does it make? You're not even here anymore," he told Luke. Then he turned to Stephanie. "And you're in the middle of running a disastrous show.

Which you fully deserve, since you got me on probation."

"I can't believe you," Luke said. "How could you let me take all the blame for what you did? Why didn't you come forward and confess you trashed the lodge when you heard I was getting kicked out?"

Keith stared at the concrete wall. For a second, he almost looked guilty. "I couldn't. You know what would happen? I'd get sent home for the summer and be stuck inside with my parents yelling at me all day. At least you still got to hang out on the lake, since you live here."

"So that's what you figured?" Luke asked. "That I wouldn't really care if you ruined my summer?"

Keith shrugged. "Sorry," he mumbled.

"Don't even say that! You're not sorry," Luke said. "And I can't wait to go upstairs right now and tell Mr. Davis and Mr. McCready everything you did!"

"Go ahead—try!" Keith scoffed. "You still don't have any evidence. They'll never believe you," he said.

There was a scuffling sound in the hallway behind Stephanie. "Think again, Keith!" Mr.

McCready stepped out of the hallway shadows. "We heard everything!"

Keith started to run, but Heather jumped right in front of him and put a hand on his chest.

"Not so fast," she said. "Mr. M and I are not about to let you get away—not after everything you've done!"

CHAPTER
15

"If everyone could bear with me for a moment," Mr. McCready said at the end of the talent show. "I have several announcements to make!"

Mr. McCready had restored power to the lodge, and the talent show had gone on as planned. The show was a big hit.

Mr. McCready tapped the microphone. "Three cheers for everyone who participated in the talent show. You were all great!"

The crowd cheered loudly. Some of the boys were standing on chairs and applauding.

"Congratulations, campers—you're all winners!" Heather added.

Stephanie grinned as she saw all of the cabins celebrating.

"Now, I'd like to thank Stephanie for doing such a great job," Mr. McCready said. "This was our first camp talent show fundraiser, and we raised nearly six hundred dollars to donate to a local girls' club! Thank you all for donating so generously," he told the audience. "We'll be happy to do the same next week at your talent show."

Mr. McCready cleared his throat. His face took on a very serious expression.

Is he going to tell everyone what happened? Stephanie scanned the crowded room for Luke. She hadn't seen him—or Keith—since Heather and Mr. McCready took them upstairs to meet with Mr. Davis. None of her friends even knew what had happened yet! She hadn't had a chance to tell them. She held her breath and awaited Mr. McCready's next words.

"Tonight, you're probably unaware of something Stephanie was dealing with," Mr. McCready continued. "It turns out that not only was there a raging thunderstorm, but the storm isn't what caused the power outage that had us all running around scared. Someone turned off all the lights—on purpose."

"What?" a young girl yelled.

"Who would do that?" a camper from Clear-water asked.

Mr. McCready stepped forward. "I'm sorry to say it was Keith Walters. And that wasn't the only thing he did to try and wreck the talent show."

Rene shuffled over beside Stephanie. "I told you it wasn't me!" she whispered fiercely.

Stephanie nodded. "I know—and I'm really sorry!" she whispered back. She and Rene exchanged friendly shrugs.

"That Keith. What a loser," Rene said as she shook her head.

Stephanie smiled.

"Keith tried some other things, but Stephanie and the CIT crew didn't let him get in the way of the show," Mr. McCready said. "But one thing Keith did succeed at was ransacking the boys' lodge a few weeks ago."

Rene turned to Stephanie with wide eyes. "You mean Luke really didn't—"

Stephanie nodded. "I told you!" she whispered.

Rene smiled ruefully. "I guess we were both wrong."

"Mr. Davis has already taken Keith to his office

to call his parents," Mr. McCready said. "Now, as you all remember, Luke Hayes was suspended from camp a few weeks ago, when we thought he was responsible for the vandalism. Well, Luke happens to be here tonight. He even helped us catch Keith. So Luke, would you mind coming up onstage?"

Stephanie's knees felt weak as she watched Luke hop up onto the stage. *This is it!* she thought. *The moment we were hoping would come!*

"Mr. Davis asked me to apologize for all of us here at the two camps. We were wrong when we accused you," Mr. McCready said.

"And we're very sorry," Heather added. "You said you were innocent, and we didn't believe you. We didn't give you a fair shake."

"We want everyone to know that Luke had nothing to do with the lodge vandalism," Mr. McCready said. "Now, Luke. Would you please return to camp for the rest of the summer? I know it's not much to offer, but—"

Luke waved Mr. McCready's concerns aside. "That's enough! I really want to come back." He glanced over at Stephanie.

"And there's one more mistake we made. We're sorry we let you go as a CIT, Stephanie," Heather said. "But if you can believe it, we were really only trying to protect you. Would you consider returning as a CIT for the rest of the summer—and please accept our apologies?"

Stephanie grinned. "I'd be really glad to go back to Loon Cabin. Thanks, Heather!"

All the girls from Loon Cabin rushed toward Stephanie and surrounded her in a massive group hug.

"Stephanie's coming back!" Marguerite cried.

"Congratulations," Vanessa told her.

"All right, everyone—thanks for a wonderful talent show. Very entertaining." Mr. McCready tipped his baseball cap to the crowd. "And I believe you know what to do next. The counselors are setting up punch and cake, and—"

"It's time to party!" Heather cried as she threw her fist awkwardly into the air.

"Does Heather know how to have fun?" Allie said as she came up to Stephanie.

"Come on, don't be so hard on her," Stephanie said. "She just gave me my job back!" She grinned as she saw the Flamingoes coming her way through the crowd.

"Guess what?" Tiffany asked in a bubbly voice as she rushed up to them. "Heather just told us we're off probation! The week's up! No more cleaning up after horses, no more dishes—"

"It's about time," Rene complained. "One more day of mucking out the stalls, and I was going to have to throw out all of my clothes."

"Was it that bad?" Stephanie asked.

"Yes!" Rene cried.

"Hey, I'm really sorry I accused you of trying to wreck the show," Stephanie said. "And you guys really did a good job on it. So, thanks," Stephanie said.

"You're welcome," Cynthia said.

"It was fun working together," Jenny conceded.

"Well, let's face it, Stephanie. You couldn't have done it without us," Rene said. "I mean, we had the talent and the experience to pull it off."

Stephanie hid a small smile. Maybe the Flamingoes *were* willing to work with us, she thought. But Rene hasn't changed one bit!

"And we really appreciate that," Stephanie told her.

"Yeah, okay, whatever. Isn't there cake somewhere?" Rene disappeared into the crowd, her friends trailing after her.

"I don't know which is weirder," Darcy said. "Us sort of getting along with the Flamingoes—or the fact it was Keith doing all that stuff!" Darcy shook her head. "I knew he liked practical jokes, but I never thought he'd go that far."

"I can't believe he'd stand by while someone else got kicked out of camp for something he did." Kayla frowned. "That's really low."

Allie smiled sheepishly at Stephanie. "Can you forgive me for giving you such a hard time about Luke? I'm really sorry, but the evidence—I mean, it all seemed like—"

"I know," Stephanie told her. "It really did look bad."

Luke came up behind Stephanie and put his arms around her waist. "It sure did. But at least Stephanie still believed in me."

"I did, too!" Anna said. "Well, until the end. Then I kind of lost it."

"Sorry, Luke. I really didn't give you a chance," Allie apologized. "I just thought . . ."

"The same thing everyone else thought." Luke let go of Stephanie. "It's okay. I understand. I'm just really glad it's all over."

"It's great you're coming back to camp!" Darcy said.

"They can totally use you down at the lake," Kayla said.

"Thanks, you guys. I appreciate that," Luke

said. "But, um, if you'll excuse me—could I get a minute alone with Stephanie?"

"Well . . ." Anna tapped her chin a few times. "Okay—if you insist." She winked at Stephanie and then turned to go. "Come on, guys, there's cake waiting for us!" They hurried off, and Luke guided Stephanie to a quiet corner, away from the crowd at the snack tables.

"I know what you're thinking," Luke said as they perched on a windowsill. "Too little too late. What a waste of a summer. Right?"

Stephanie shook her head. "I wasn't thinking that at all. I was thinking how great it is that we have two more weeks to hang out together!"

"I can't thank you enough, Stephanie." Luke reached out and touched Stephanie's cheek. "You completely went to bat for me. You camped out on this floor. You crawled around Keith's cabin, you stood up to Heather, you lost your CIT position—"

"It was nothing," Stephanie said with a wave of her hand.

"Come on. I don't believe that!" Luke laughed.

"Oh. Well, then, maybe you'll believe this. I'm so glad you're here! It was worth whatever it took."

Luke grinned. "So when do you want to learn how to water-ski? I was thinking tomorrow morning—meet me down at the boathouse at around six?"

Stephanie playfully swatted his arm. "No way! I don't want to be boring, but I think we'd better do everything by the rules from now on."

"You have a point," Luke told her. "Oh well, it was worth a shot."

Stephanie smiled at Luke. "And this summer was worth all the trouble—because I got to know you." She reached for Luke's hand. "Now come on—the cake's almost gone!"

WIN A $500 SHOPPING SPREE AT THE WARNER BROTHERS STUDIO STORE!

1 Grand Prize: A $500 shopping spree at the Warner Brothers Studio Store

---

Complete entry form and send to: Pocket Books/ "Full House Club Stephanie Sweepstakes"
1230 Avenue of the Americas, 13th Floor, NY, NY 10020

NAME _____ **BIRTHDATE** ___/___/___

ADDRESS _____

CITY _____ **STATE** _____ **ZIP** _____

PHONE (_____) _____

PARENT OR LEGAL GUARDIAN'S SIGNATURE *(required for entrants under 18 years of age at date of entry.)*

_____

See back for official rules.

Pocket Books/ "Full House Club Stephanie Sweepstakes"
Sponsors Official Rules:

No Purchase Necessary.

Enter by mailing this completed Official Entry Form (no copies allowed) or by mailing a 3" x 5" card with your name and address, daytime telephone number and birthdate to the Pocket Books/ "Full House Club Stephanie Sweepstakes", 1230 Avenue of the Americas, 13th Floor, NY, NY 10020. Entry forms are available in the back of Full House Club Stephanie #10: Truth or Dare (6/00), #11: Summertime Secrets (7/00) and #12: The Real Thing (8/00), on in-store book displays and on the web site SimonSaysKids.com. Sweepstakes begins 6/1/00. Entries must be postmarked by 8/31/00 and received by 9/15/00. Sponsors are not responsible for lost, late, damaged, postage-due, stolen, illegible, mutilated, incomplete, or misdirected or not delivered entries or mail or for typographical errors in the entry form or rules or for telecommunications system or computer software or hardware errors or data loss. Entries are void if they are in whole or in part illegible, incomplete or damaged. Enter as often as you wish, but each entry must be mailed separately. Winner will be selected at random from all eligible entries received in a drawing to be held on or about 9/25/00. The Winner will be notified by phone.

Prizes: One Prize: A $500 shopping spree at the Warner Brothers Studio Store. (retail value: $500).

The sweepstakes is open to legal residents of the U.S. (excluding Puerto Rico) and Canada (excluding Quebec) ages 6-10 as of 8/31/00. Proof of age is required to claim prize. Prize will be awarded to the winner's parent or legal guardian. Void wherever prohibited or restricted by law. All federal, state and local laws apply. Simon & Schuster, Inc., Parachute Publishing, Warner Bros. and their respective officers, directors, shareholders, employees, suppliers, parent companies, subsidiaries, affiliates, agencies, sponsors, participating retailers, and persons connected with the use, marketing or conduct of this sweepstakes are not eligible. Family members living in the same household as any of the individuals referred to in the preceding sentence are not eligible.

Prize is not transferable and may not be substituted except by sponsors, in the event of prize unavailability, in which case a prize of equal or greater value will be awarded. The odds of winning the prize depend upon the number of eligible entries received.

If the winner is a Canadian resident, then he/she must correctly answer a skill-based question administered by mail.

All expenses on receipt and use of prize including federal, state and local taxes are the sole responsibility of the winner. Winner's parents or legal guardians may be required to execute and return an Affidavit of Eligibility and Publicity Release and all other legal documents which the sweepstakes sponsors may require (including a W-9 tax form) within 15 days of attempted notification or an alternate winner may be selected.

Winner or winner's parents or legal guardians on winner's behalf agree to allow use of winner's name, photograph, likeness, and entry for any advertising, promotion and publicity purposes without further compensation to or permission from the entrant, except where prohibited by law.

Winner and winner's parents or legal guardians agree that Simon & Schuster, Inc., Parachute Publishing and Warner Bros. and their respective officers, directors, shareholders, employees, suppliers, parent companies, subsidiaries, affiliates, agencies, sponsors, participating retailers, and persons connected with the use, marketing or conduct of this sweepstakes, shall have no responsibility or liability for injuries, losses or damages of any kind in connection with the collection, acceptance or use of the prize awarded herein, or from participation in this promotion.

By participating in this sweepstakes, entrants agree to be bound by these rules and the decisions of the judges and sweepstakes sponsors, which are final in all matters relating to the sweepstakes. Failure to comply with the Official Rules may result in a disqualification of your entry and prohibition of any further participation in this sweepstakes.

The first name of the winner will be posted at SimonSaysKids.com or the first name of the winner may be obtained by sending a stamped, self-addressed envelope after 9/31/00 to Prize Winners, Pocket Books "Full House Club Stephanie Sweepstakes," 1230 Avenue of the Americas, 13th Floor, NY, NY 10020.

TM & © 2000 Warner Bros.

**Don't miss out on any of
Stephanie and Michelle's
exciting adventures!**

FULL HOUSE™

SISTERS

*When sisters get together...
expect the unexpected!*

A MINSTREL® BOOK

Published by Pocket Books

2012-04

FULL HOUSE™
Michelle

A MINSTREL® BOOK
Published by Pocket Books
™ & © 2000 Warner Bros. All Rights Reserved.   1033-32